FLAMINGO LAND

and Other Stories

Edited by

Ellah Wakatama Allfrey

Flight Press

An Imprint of Spread the Word

First published in Great Britain in 2015 by
Flight Press, an imprint of Spread the Word
Unit 6, The Albany
Douglas Way
London
SE8 4AG

www.spreadtheword.org.uk

ISBN 9780954008352
Typeset in London by Spread the Word
Cover design by Mark Ecob

CONTENTS

ACKNOWLEDGEMENTS

With generous thanks to Arts Council England and Esmée Fairbairn Foundation for their support and extraordinary belief in Spread the Word and in Flight 1000.

Huge thanks to Flight Associates Jennifer Obidike, Len Lukowski and Sanya Semakula, whose energy and vision was key in shaping this anthology.

Thanks also to former director of Spread the Word Sue Lawther. To Paul Sherreard, who makes things happen so warmly and conscientiously (and who, at the time this is being written, is boarding a plane to the US for a few months. Gratefully, this enables us to name and thank him, as his modesty would never have allowed for such an acknowledgement.)

To the stellar editorial team of Ellah Wakatama Allfrey and Vimbai Shire, thank you.

Thanks to the talented short story writers, whose unique voices make *Flamingo Land* an exciting and vibrant place.

And finally, thanks to all those who read this anthology and to the extended family of Spread the Word.

FOREWORD

At Spread the Word, we love it when we come across work we want to bring to an audience, from new and emerging writers that deserve attention. Whether it's through competitions, recommendations, chats at our events and workshops or by other means, we encounter a lot of good stuff, and it's a pleasure when we are able to provide a platform, via our imprint Flight Press, for some of the best of what we have seen.

This book brings together the winning and short-listed stories from the London Short Story Prize 2014 in a collection that includes other stories that have caught our imaginations, from writers we think you will want to find out more about. We are excited that this book contains the work of writers from lots of different backgrounds; each voice here is different to the next, and each voice has its own 'truth' which rings out through the work. This is refreshing for a form that can sometimes seem dominated by a certain kind of tone and content.

As well as being proud of the writing within this book, we are proud of the hard work and talents of the editorial team of Len Lukowski, Jennifer Obidike and Sanya Semakula who took this book through its production, working closely with the editor Ellah Allfrey and copy editor Vimbai Shire. Len, Jennifer and Sanya are developing their careers in publishing through Spread the Word's Flight 1000 programme, which helps talented people from under-represented backgrounds gain experience, contacts and routes into the industry. This book is just one of a number of things they have achieved in their year on the scheme.

We think it's a truly diverse collection of new and compelling writing, produced by a fresh and interesting editorial crew. We hope you enjoy reading it!

Paul Sherreard
Spread the Word

EDITOR'S NOTE

Where do stories come from?

In this collection, you, dear reader, will find several tales in which the setting is a side-step from reality. There are also characters who will seem startlingly familiar – or at the very least, believable. From the heightened atmosphere of an art studio to the harsh realities of life at the poverty line, the writers featured in *Flamingo Land and Other Stories* explore that very human need for agency, the desire to feel some control over our own existence, to understand why we are here and what it is we are meant to be doing.

Stephanie Victoire presents a fearless protofeminist heroine in her fairy tale, 'Layla and the Axe'; Ruby Cowling's 'Flamingo Land' conjures an all-too believable near future in which the most basic bodily needs are monitored by the state; in 'The Passenger', Katie Willis chronicles domestic violence and imagines the possibility of escape with deceptively lyrical prose. Sanya Semakula's 'Purple Haze' is a story of loss and identity, and the difficulties of maintaining relationships in a new country. All four of these stories examine the nature of family and its survival. Two very different middle-aged women assert their identities in Colette Sensier's 'Mrs Świętokrzyskie's Castle' and Janet H Swinney's 'The Works of Lesser-Known Artists', while Jennifer Obidike's 'Still Life', Uschi Gatward's 'On Margate Sands' and Shaun Levin's 'The Man in the Pool' meditate on art, memory and meaning.

This is where good stories come from: writers observing the world *and* looking within to conjure characters, places and plots that interrogate the universal through the specific. And, more importantly, in an age beset with so many possible distractions, this is how good stories find their readers: when writers are brought together with initiatives such as Spread the Word who identify, nurture and promote work that has something important to say. Each author featured here has been part of a Spread the Word writer's initiative. There's a kind of alchemy that happens when writer meets publisher, meets editor. I feel very lucky to have been part of that this year and hope you enjoy the results.

Ellah Wakatama Allfrey, OBE

Layla and the Axe

Stephanie Victoire

Layla trudges through the grass, across the meadow towards the forest, with Rowan by her side and the axe weighing heavy in her hand. 'He won't get me. He won't get me,' she mutters to herself over and over, chanting. She swats away a fly without looking at it. Summer buzzes all around her in the stiff heat that renders birds, bees and butterflies restless. Rowan trots along, his brush hanging low behind him, his thin legs keeping up with his friend's.

The axe that Layla carries is not clean and isn't new; it has cracked its way through logs and it has threatened a wife who didn't know how to stop her mouth. It has sat in the corner by the hearth, watching a chubby white cat writhe on the fraying rug and young, excitable girls spill tea on the sofa. It has seen snow being stamped off of heavy boots and a mother sob hearty tears when the rest of the house was sleeping. And now this axe might very well be a hero. Layla has a small bruise forming on her knee from where she buckled over the locked gate and landed awkwardly and hard onto the gravel before reaching the pale greens and dry yellows of the meadow's floor. She had brushed herself down and waited for Rowan to squeeze through the gap, tucking his body in and making himself flat. His ears warn Layla of sounds she has yet to hear. One of his ears was scraped and scabby when she first found him.

'You're my fox now aren't you?' she'd said softly, dabbing hot lavender water over the wound with a flannel, the fragrant steam rising from the bowl and dampening her skin. Rowan, who was just called 'Fox' then, was shaking and contemplating whether he should stay with this girl or bolt through the kitchen door and back through the hole in the garden where he came from. 'You're my fox now. You chose me.' Layla was prepared for the telling-off she knew she was in for when Pa got home. 'Get that thing out of here! Do you know what diseases they carry?' Pa yelled when he came into the kitchen and saw the woodland animal shifting nervously in Layla's embrace. Pa was tall and broad – a giant even – but Layla already knew that even the smallest of creatures could stand up to a giant.

The trees now appear plentiful and stretch their branches up high. Layla thinks of Alice watching the room grow tall around her. 'Drink me,' she says aloud, neither to herself nor to Rowan. Her mouth pushes out words to take her mind off the heaviness in her grasp.

He got to Sylvia in the spring, this monster in the forest. With her cardigan torn and a smudge of soil on her cheek, she ran straight to her mother, who now bolts her front door at sundown.

'He kissed me,' Sylvia whispered to Layla when they met one morning under the birch tree. 'He gave me biscuits and buns and a mug of hot tea.'

Rowan tucked in his wiry tail and curled up at Layla's feet.

'So why are you crying if he gave you such treats?' Layla asked, her stomach now grumbling for the blueberry pie Ma sometimes made.

'Because he kissed me, Layla. He kissed me and his fingers crept up my thigh.'

Sylvia had escaped with a kick to his knee and tugged her cardigan until it slipped from his clammy hand. She fell in the dirt just outside his house and thought for sure she'd never make it home.

'Who is he?' Layla asked, not sure if Sylvia was telling the truth. Layla had known everyone who'd lived in the village all the thirteen years of her life and had been going into the forest since she was seven and not once had she seen a tiny cottage anywhere in there, let alone a man who lived inside it.

But Layla and everyone else in the village believed it enough when Melody, Mrs Hanigan's daughter, hadn't been so lucky on Midsummer's Eve. It had started out as a happy celebration. Everyone was gathered outside except for Sylvia and her mother, who'd closed their curtains and locked themselves in for the night. The grown-ups were merry on cider and Mr Finn made a fire pit. Rowan skittered away from it at first, until Layla began to dance around the flames with her sister, Allie, and soon Rowan looked like he was dancing too, hopping back and forth between the two girls, his orange tail puffing out in excitement.

'See if you can spot the faeries, girls,' Mrs Hanigan said to all the daughters. Her cheeks were rosy with cheer. She pointed to a cluster of trees at the mouth of the forest. 'They come out on this night especially. Go see, go see!'

Melody ran ahead, her yellow dress and flower garland disappearing into the black.

'Get a torch, for goodness' sake! And don't go too deep. Just at the brink there.' Pa put his big, dry hand on Layla's shoulder to stop her from running off.

'I know where Pa keeps his torch,' Allie said, tearing off towards the house with her long dark hair sailing behind her like a cape. But Melody didn't wait for the others and she didn't come back to them that night. Layla asked Rowan to go and find Melody, but he wouldn't leave her side. Allie wouldn't help her look either; she was distracted, saying that she was sure she'd just seen little dots of lights circling the bluebells.

'Those must have been the faeries, like Mrs Hanigan said!' Layla saw nothing out there in the forest and went to bed feeling uneasy.

That joy she had seen in Mrs Hanigan's eyes was gone for good when Melody returned the next morning and said that some man in the forest had forced her to make a baby. Everyone's pa and uncles and brothers marched into the forest that day but came back perplexed and anguished; neither the cottage nor the man could be found.

Layla's shoulder now aches and she must stop to take a moment's rest. She crouches down on her haunches, lets the axe slip from her aching palm and Rowan circles her, sniffing at the boots Pa gave her. They are slightly too big but he insists they will last a lifetime, and so Layla fills them with thick, knitted socks. Her small, flat feet throb in these boots now. Layla hears a rustle between her jagged breaths, but Rowan must have heard it some seconds before, as he is on his way towards a moss-caked log to inspect it. Layla stands up again and turns her head up to the sky, where the sun is pouring down its light. Layla takes it in her arms as if it will charge her with power.

'He won't get me and he'll never get Allie.'

It was the evening before, the height of the harvest moon, when Allie thought she might find the faerie folk again. 'I thought this night was special too,' Allie had explained through tears, her forearm sore from where Ma had dragged her back to the house.

'You're not to go in there ever again! Is that understood?' Ma said in a tone they had never heard from her before, her words escaping through gritted teeth. Pa was resting deep in bed upstairs and no one would tell him about Allie running across the meadow. Earlier that evening, Rowan had nipped at Layla's ankles to warn her of her sister's absence. It took Layla only seconds to realise that something was wrong. Layla and Ma burst through the door and sprinted across the meadow like two cheetahs. Layla lost her breath first. Ma found Allie at the start of the forest, where Layla finds herself now. Allie had whispered to Layla as they lay nose to nose in bed that night, that there was a man with a big smile who was coming towards her just before Ma arrived.

Layla strides on and Rowan bounds out from behind the log, abandoning his inspection of what is most likely squirrels rustling to join her, and deeper into the forest they go.

'He won't get me with smiles. He won't get me with sweets. I'll take his head clean off before he can touch me.' The further in they go, the thicker the smell of pine and moss gets. She smells the various flowers and the earthiness of the trees and on any other day, Layla would want to take this forest in fragrance and bottle it. But today she is looking for the rot in the forest, the poison trying to choke anything that comes near it.

'Where is he?' Layla says and looks down at Rowan, whose eyes squint in the sunlight, looking like two thin streaks of black ink.

Layla looks back to check which path they've

taken and hopes that they can find their way back out. They walk on into the belly of the forest, where the sunlight is stolen away. The hairs on Layla's arm prickle. Rowan's fur moves a little in the breeze. The greens around them grow dark – and up ahead – Layla catches a wink of a red-coloured roof between branches. She has definitely been in this part of the forest before and this cottage was never here. Layla stops walking and so does Rowan.

'That's his house there, Rowan. We're here.' She switches the axe from her aching left hand to her still-strong right and they each place one foot carefully in front of the other towards the front steps. A few birds chirp and the chimney puffs and Layla believes she can smell blueberries. The air feels thicker and warmer with the burning of a stove, she can feel its heat through the half-open window. A pale-blue curtain flutters and Layla draws her breath up heartily into her lungs. Rowan sniffs at the steps, his black triangular ears bobbing up and down. Sweat drops from Layla's forehead and into her eyes, stinging them for a moment. She can hear her own pulse, she can smell her own sweaty skin, but she moves her lips to chant again, silently, 'He won't get me. He won't get me.' But Rowan can hear her; his ear darts backwards and the tip of his nose twitches.

'Hello?' a voice calls invitingly from behind the orange-painted door.

Layla raises the axe like she's seen Pa do.

Rowan crouches low with his legs slightly spread. 'Come in! Come in!' says the voice again and, at the turning of the handle and the creak of the door, Layla pushes through the aches in her arms, ready to swing, and thinks Pa's axe could be a hero.

Flamingo Land

Ruby Cowling

The stained concrete of the big Procedure Unit building made it look as if it might, at least, once have been a real hospital. It was one of the okay ones, -ish – the waiting times weren't bad, and I knew the best place to park because it was right behind the FHO where we went for Assessment.

I scraped the dirty slush off my trainers, went in and gave Mum's name, and they sent me up to the third floor. I found her near the end of the ward, half-propped on a bottom bunk, looking at an old *Gourmet* magazine.

'How you feeling?'

'Oh, Tommy love. At last. Let's get gone before they bring that sandwich trolley.' She was obviously thinking straight, though she was slurring a bit. 'Have you had anything?'

It went without saying, I hadn't. Trying to avoid her dressings, I helped her into her clothes and into the wheelchair; she was so light. She gave a little wave to everyone as I wheeled her out.

Driving home, I glanced across to see she was

snoozing, her head thrown back, mouth open wide like a hungry chick, and I put the radio on quiet. I'd been the family driver since I turned seventeen, Dad presenting me with the keys to our old Sharan as if he couldn't wait to get in the back with Beth and the twins. It'd been the same with the bills and stuff. One parents' evening the school mentioned me maybe doing Maths AS-level early, and that weekend Dad handed over all his piles of paper and a notebook on which he'd written: PASSWORDS/PIN NUMBERS, and clapped me on the shoulder like I was finally becoming a man.

The kitchen was cold but felt freshly deserted, the tang of pickled onion Monster Munch staining the air. I knew it was hard for Beth to stop the twins: one would help the other onto the worktop to reach the cupboards, and I'd even come in once to find Kenny grilling cheese on toast like a little expert. It was all the cooking programmes they watched. I didn't like putting Beth in that adult role, especially as she benefited from me being around too – in terms of rules, keeping to them, and cupboards, keeping out of them.

I wheeled Mum through to the stair lift so she could go and have a lie down. We got a grant for the Stannah when she had the leg off – she'd filled in the forms in advance so all Dad had to do was send them in, and a couple of months later it was installed, helpful as anything.

Beth heard me put the kettle on and shouted from the telly room that she wanted two sugars. Two notes on the table: Dear Parent or Guardian, a pre-Easter-holidays trip next month, only £27.50 per child. I'd have to hide these quickly in my desk – the sideboard – otherwise they'd see them and start hoping, and I'd have another of those conversations to look forward to: Lily sniffing and wobbling, Kenny kicking the skirting board.

Dad's key turned in the door and he came in, smiling.

'Alright, Tom. Premium Bonds come up, have they?'

'Yeah, right. Just school letters.'

'Your Mum alright?'

'Oh, you know.'

Dad nodded, as if this was good. We'd been through four previous ops with Mum and this one wasn't the worst, but he never seemed worried enough. Surely even he could see she must be running out of things – you only had to look at her, or lift her. After the first couple, once she admitted they'd been elective, she'd shown us all the stuff she'd read about the redundancy built into the human body – there's a surprising amount you can survive without – and told us how glad she was to be doing something. 'Make a bit of money, help someone in need – losing a few pounds is the icing on the cake!' I realised she must like feeling aligned with You First: the element of sacrifice, doing the right thing, taking personal responsibility.

I never let myself ask Dad if, one day, he might volunteer.

'Daddy!' Lily hurled herself across the kitchen and into his arms.

'Daddy, Daddy!' Kenny shouted, 'Flamingo Land!'

Oh *shit*.

'What about Flamingo Land?' he said, grabbing one in each arm and mashing their small faces against his chest.

'There's a school trip! Everyone in the whole world's going.'

'Well, isn't everyone in the whole world lucky?'

I turned to deal with the boiling kettle, got everyone's favourite mugs lined up.

'Kenny, Lily,' I said, calling them out from under Dad's armpits. 'What kind of twins are you again?' They shrieked and piled over each other to get out and upstairs.

We had this thing: I'd say, or trick them into saying, *non-identical*, and they'd walk into it every time because they took it so seriously – who they were, how they came to be – and then I'd dive at them, fingers first, saying, *What? What? Noniden-TICKLE?* I didn't even have to say the full thing any more. It killed me the way they squealed and squirmed.

Beth filled the doorway as they scrambled up the stairs. She was wearing those peach-coloured trousers she just wouldn't give up on. She tugged the crotch away from herself when she saw me wince.

'Mum texted to say she'll just have it black.' At Christmas we'd drawn lots to see who could have the phones, and the winners were Mum and Beth.

"kay. Do you still want sugar?'

'Yes. Why?'

I stirred it in for her, handed over the two mugs. 'Let me know if she wants anything else.'

'Obvs.' She sloped back into the telly room. We used to call it the living room, and we used to mute the telly when the adverts came on, and we'd eat together at the table with Radio 4 on and talk about current affairs and get the dictionary out if somebody asked what something meant, but we kind of let all that go when Grandma finally died.

I put Dad's mug in front of him.

'Don't get them all excited. It's nearly sixty quid.'

'Ach– '

He has this habit of waving away complete impossibilities as if they're just bad smells.

'We can't . . .' I started.

'Tom, son, don't be so . . . We're going to have a good month this time. I can feel it. Look at me!'

He stood and pulled his shirt against his torso, sucking in air, and crabbed his arms like a bodybuilder. A curve of ribs, a hollow, the shock of his belt buckle.

'Dad.'

'I'm down a whole notch, you know. At work I have to sit on a cushion.' He winked. 'The future's bright, kiddo. Go on, do your sum thingies, just see what comes out. You can put me down for a straight sixty. Yes! I reckon, don't you? Then with your Mum, I mean, the swelling and that'll be gone by Monday, she can't come out more than, what, forty-five now, can she? And then there's, there's . . . '

He trailed off when his thoughts reached the four of us. He dropped his voice. 'How's Beth?'

Beth — well. The old Beth was under there somewhere, the one I used to bounce on the trampoline which now sat at 45 degrees in the tangle of our back yard, but I hadn't heard that laugh of hers for months. These days she'd just sit, texting, with this furious air about her, jagged lines daggering around her head. And as she widened into her teens she was really becoming a problem, Formula-wise. I'd seen the tiny nuggets of Creme Egg foil in our bin; I'd come in to join her watching telly, glimpsed her stuffing something down the side of the settee. It was the secrecy that got to me; that feeling she wasn't, somehow, on our team. She should have worked out already that it's just better for everyone if you go by the rules. I admit it, I had my own habits: at work I'd pick the biggest jacket potato I could see, smush a load of butter into it and get beans *and* cheese if I got the right dinner lady. But I was so hungry all the time. Don't teenage boys need more food than, like, anyone? And I'm not being funny, but unlike the clothes straining to cover the surface of Beth, mine had leeway.

But I didn't want to get into it with Dad. 'Well, Assessment's this Monday coming, so . . .'

I took my tea through to the telly room. The

screen flaunted a close-up of a fork dividing a golden sponge pudding to release a melting centre, a velvety voice-over saying how good it was. I saw Beth stiffen. She was plopped low in the cushions, chewing the rope of her hair, one hank of thigh slumped over the other. Someone would have to say something, but no one wanted to tell her directly; I definitely didn't, Dad would never shake himself into it, and Mum – well, Mum would rather have another thing removed. Still, if Dad was right and he was coming in under sixty kilos . . . maybe it wouldn't have to be this month, or next month – maybe we could hold out until April and the planned Threshold Change, before the shit hit the fan. Before Special Measures.

Two nights after, Dad came in and shook my arm, whispering so he wouldn't wake the twins in their bunks. 'What's the number now for a doctor?'

I told him the new out-of-hours medical advice number. He rang it, eyes on me, but there was a message saying it had closed down, phone your GP. The GP's message gave us their opening hours and advised ringing the new medical advice number. Dad phoned back, hoping we'd misunderstood, and I sat in the bathroom holding Mum's hair as she leaned from her wheelchair over the loo. I could feel the heat coming off her. She retched and groaned; with her new stitches every gip must have been a knife stabbing.

'Should this be happening?' said Dad from the doorway.

She finished throwing up and sat shivering. I turned away while Dad stripped off her soaking nightie and wrapped her twice round in a bath towel, then we lifted her into the aquability shower.

I knew we hadn't used up all of February's Internet credit so, with Dad keeping an eye on Mum, I dug out the Procedure Unit's scribbled discharge papers so I could look up exactly what she'd had done. They were a mess; their big thing was patient choice, and they were great at helping customers with self-directed healthcare, but they weren't so brilliant at the admin side. I went down to the kitchen, to my sideboard, and Googled *problems post-hysterectomy*, *partial hepatectomy*, *cholecystectomy*. Antibiotics seemed like the first option. I'd pop down to Anwar's before work and order them. I had an old prescription I'd managed not to use.

If she was still like this in a couple of days, though, we wouldn't make it to Assessment. Not the end of the world — you could miss one a year, enter your own provisional data — but it meant I'd have to calculate the official Formula myself.

Even unofficially doing the Formula gave me a headache. Mid-month, I'd get out the Guide and the calculator and plug in our info, see where we were. I'd chivvy the twins to get on the scales — worst of three I'd take — and get a written note from Beth, after asking about a million times. She only gave in because she knew Assessment would reveal everything anyway, and we'd had enough bad scenes after a surprise result, all of us sniping blame, storming through the waiting area past other anxious, dehydrated families. We'd drive back in silence, staring out at the golden arches, the Wild Bean Cafes, the ten-metre hoardings sighing *eat, eat* – but not stopping, because we didn't have the spare calories, and now we wouldn't have the spare cash.

The online timer told me I had a while still and, I admit it, I thought about looking at some of the sites I used to go on a lot last year. The videos. But I heard Mum retching again which was kind of a mood killer, so instead I went to the tax office website to check for Formula updates. You never knew: an early Threshold Change, maybe. But no. I logged in to college to see how far behind I was. Then email, but no surprise pay rise announcement from work, ha ha, and no secret admirer messages from fit local girls, ha even more ha. Finally I went to look at the news, because Mum never let us have it on the telly. Dad appeared behind me as I read.

'Oh dear,' he said in that sad way, like it was people he knew, people down the road. 'There's always someone worse off, eh?' And he gave my shoulder a squeeze. I turned, so he'd stop.

'Well,' he said, 'Your mum's settled down. Better get to sleep myself if I'm to be up and at 'em tomorrow, eh?'

Something flared up in me as he ambled out. His relentless happy-man good humour. He never seemed to stop and question his life, our tiny terrace, the state of Mum, his embarrassing job. He used to teach art history at the uni. All his family had been teachers or doctors or whatever but something had happened, and it was like he couldn't get back to where he was before. Grandma used to call it *a little local difficulty* and change the subject.

I'd only ever heard Dad say, *There's a lot of competition out there; a man can't expect to be on top all his life; I'm lucky to even have a job;* blah blah. *It means I can focus on my book.* His 'book', as he calls it, sits on the shelf above my sideboard in a lever arch file. I'd never seen him touch it, though I remember him a few years ago shut in the bedroom during the day, Mum saying he was trying to write. I suppose we were living on his redundancy then – I was only eleven, I didn't think about it – and then Mum got her little surprise, then the bigger surprise that there were two of them, and it all coincided with the rollout of You First, which I remember because of all the announcements at school about the changes, and then the Formula came in. So he had to find something; he couldn't really keep waiting to go back. But then he seemed to forget things had been any other way. We struggled month after month and Dad just said, *Ah well. We do our best. No fault of our own.* Maybe not, but he never thought about whose fault it was, or what we might do about it.

I was starving. I went back to bed.

After dropping Beth and the twins at their schools I headed to Anwar's, but although it was going on for nine, his shutters were still down. We'd been using Drugworld for a while because it was next to the big Asda, but I'd stopped at Anwar's for paracetamol a few weeks ago and he was open then. I got a lucky parking space and sat looking at the dead shop. Anwar was never exactly joyful, especially since they'd lost a granddaughter to a family of vegans in Colne, but last time I saw him he looked really grim, told me Drugworld had put in some official query about his dispensing licence. *Troublemakers*, he said. *Bullshit merchants.* It sounded funny in his accent, funny coming from that kind face.

I drove off to the retail park. Drugworld, so brightly lit, had the biggest range of everything you can imagine. A relief: Mum would get what she needed today. The price, though. After I paid I had to sit down for a minute on the old people's plastic waiting chairs. I must have had my head in my hands or whatever, because I didn't see Erin until she was standing right in front of me saying my name in this concerned way.

'Oh,' I said, sitting up.

'Alright?'

' . . . Yeah.'

'I'm just getting . . .' She lifted her basket – four different flavours of SlimFast, which no way did Erin need.

'Right. I had to get some stuff for my mum.'

'She have another op?'

'Yeah.'

'Huh, wow.' She fiddled with the stuff in her basket. 'How's Beth?'

'Alright. You know.'

She nodded. We said nothing for a minute.

'So how's college? Top of the class?' she said, jaunting out one hip.

'Ha, yeah. Well, actually not really.'

'Come on.'

'No, I haven't gone for ages, had extra shifts and that.'

'I bet you'll get all As anyway, with your big maths brain. You love all that stuff, don't you?'

Some old woman with a crutch came up, aiming herself at my seat.

'Well, I'd better . . .'

'Yeah.'

'See you.'

I watched her walk off towards the self-checkouts. Erin hardly looked at me usually, even after last June, when it was boiling and I helped her revise for her exams, lying on the grass outside her flat, and her boyfriend had turned up on his bike and she told him she was going to be busy all day and he zoomed off and she nudged me in the side and I'd not said anything. Especially after last June, actually.

Mum started to get better after a week or so, but we'd missed Assessment. So after work on the last day of February, instead of going to college, I sat at the sideboard and did the Formula.

One evening when the Formula first came in I found Dad hunched over the You First Family Guide, close to tears. Amongst other stuff the Guide helps you make your own Action Plan to pass Assessment, and it includes the actual Formula they use. I sat down and had a look, tried to explain it. Each family member gets a number of points, depending how they compare against the national average, given on tables in the back of the Guide. You add them all together and you get a number, W, which you plug in to the Formula:

$$\frac{W}{(N+A)} * (1 - \frac{((N-3)*INT(\frac{1.1}{(1+2^{-N})}))}{N}) + 25*(A-2)$$

Where N is the number of children, A the number of adults and so on – obvious. There's a penalty for one-parent families, and – hard cheese for us – a penalty for having more than three children. Dad rang up to double-check about the twins, because he couldn't believe they really counted as two, but they did. I could see the logic both ways.

If you achieve your ideal weights, you get your full amount, but if you fail it's cut, really cut. Then if you keep on failing, Special Measures. Maybe it was seeing how close we were getting that had made Dad cry.

I finished, and sat for a minute with my eyes closed. I'd have to go online to enter the final figures, but first I got myself a filling glass of water and joined the others in the telly room. The usual repeats were on: a young Jamie Oliver was pounding a massive steak through some cling film with a rolling pin. When he'd finished, beaming, the ads came: stuffed crusts oozing mozzarella, buckets of crispy chicken. Then came one of those low-quality montage adverts, showing stills of local Easter attractions: the model railway, the mining museum, the petting zoo.

'So,' said Dad. 'Flamingo Land.'

'Dad . . . '

I couldn't believe him. A fortnight ago I'd said no – Lily had cried for two hours – but they'd moved on, the twins, and accepted it. Now they sat up and looked at each other as if they'd heard Santa's sleigh bells.

'Oh Tom,' he waved me away. 'Let them tell me about it.'

Kenny panted down his mouthful of 5 Alive. 'It's the whole of Year Three, it's like a whole day and we have to go in a coach at six o'clock in the morning!'

'It's half past six it sets off, Kenny,' said serious Lily. 'But Tom said we couldn't go.'

'Well,' said Mum from the corner, looking at me. 'Let's see. It's a whole day? Won't you need a packed lunch? And a bit of spending money?'

Kenny was already shaking his head, his eyes wide. 'Nope, there's this place there where the children go to eat – they have crocodile soup and pelican pie and like, armadillo something, I can't remember, but you get this like voucher for the shop too, and Miss said to tell our mums and dads it was all inclu— inclusied.'

Mum and Dad glanced at each other. The twins jumped to the edge of their seats.

'Tommy?' said Dad, 'How's it looking?'

I drank some water, tried to steady myself. 'Well, I put all the numbers in –'

'Did you put me in at sixty?'

'Yeah, sixty dead on, and Mum at forty-five –'

'Oh, I don't even know if I'm that, now,' said Mum, and she went into this coughing fit. Beth got up and rubbed her back for her.

'But, you know how complicated it is, and I mean, we're all still growing, even me . . .'

I was trying so hard not to look at Beth.

'So,' Dad said, 'what did you come up with? We'll get our full lot this month, won't we?'

'I can't – I don't know exactly.'

Then Lily turned her small face up to me. 'Is it . . . So are we still not going?'

Seal pup eyes.

It felt so nice to log in to the account and see a positive figure. It felt amazing to be able to tell the twins they could go on their trip, to send them off to school with the money and the signed tear-off slips in their little backpacks. And it felt completely new to have two purple twenties in my wallet, to actually plan for real how I was going to ask Erin if she fancied a drink sometime, maybe even a Pizza Express.

And then somehow it just ebbed away. Dad a bit freer with his debit card; Mum's internet bits and bobs she'd been waiting to get; cash for store-cupboard stuff; petrol at Asda; shoes for Kenny and Lily; the standing orders; bit by bit each day it dwindled, and then it was all gone.

In the Family Health Office there was a big green poster headed: *You First presents the Fantastic FORMULA for Family Fitness!* Clip-art party hats and streamers either side of the header, and a graph. I stood up to have a proper look. Then I felt my face go red before I realised why – there was this scent I recognised, and I turned round and it was Erin with her sisters and her mum.

'Wow – hi.'

'Don't normally see you,' she said.

'They changed our day. Because of Mum, the other week?'

'How's she doing?'

'Better. Thanks. You going in?'

'Yep, when they call us.'

'What do you think?' I nodded toward the Assessment room.

'Oh yeah, we're well under. What about you? Did you have to do it yourself?'

'Should be good, should be fine, it worked out okay, it looked – yeah.' Nodding and nodding, toeing the nylon carpet.

'Pain, innit? It does work, though.' She nodded toward the graph and its downslope. 'Says the average has gone way down.'

It was like a silver bell in my brain. But there was another thing biting at me: *now or never Tom or you are an utter waste of space.* 'Look, I wanted to ask you something, are you, would you –'

'Taylor-Peel?'

We were being called in. It was the Assessor with the ankles and the shiny hair down the back of her white coat, and I admit it, I didn't want to keep her waiting.

Someone had left one of those tipping trolleys full of plastic crates on the wheelchair ramp, so me and Dad carried Mum down the steps. It was snowing again, settling on the slope of daffodils behind the rank of cars. Kenny and Lily bundled each other through the revolving door like they had when we'd come in, but quiet. With a jerk of my head I got them to follow us. Beth was already at the car, jabbing at her phone. I admit I looked at her phone once when she was in the loo. The texts she sent to about twenty different friends were long and witty, full of smileys. They'd shocked me more than I'd been expecting.

I wasn't going to be the first one to speak. Whatever I said, Beth would say I was having a go at her. And, well, it sort of was her fault. She was the one who cost us so much in food, the one who just kept getting heavier like she didn't care. Someone was going to have to say something.

I said nothing. We set off on the ring road, first drop-off the twins' school.

The fit Assessor had handed me an updated Family Guide. It was true: average weights were down; the points tables had been adjusted. Erin was still in the waiting room as we left, and I wanted to stop and say, hang on, think about it, if there's been a drop in average weights wouldn't everyone who was doing just about okay suddenly be above average? And then fail Assessment? But of course it couldn't work that way, surely, that would be stupid. And I'd remembered her mouth twisting when she said about my big maths brain. And then the Assessor had gone to unbolt the double doors for Mum's chair and she'd bent over and I couldn't not look.

Of all people, it was Dad, sitting in the middle seat, who spoke. 'I s'pose we have to, then.'

I still didn't say anything.

'Can we, Tom? Can we pay it back?'

We couldn't really, no.

Dad was quiet for a while.

He shook his head. 'It doesn't make sense. Not at all.'

Beth in the far back seat pulled out her earbuds. 'Well, it's not just me.'

'Course not, lovey,' he said. 'No one said it was your fault.'

'You don't have to say it, though.' She was

rattling the seats in front of her, almost standing. 'I can see the way you all look at me, like I'm the problem. Like you want me to die.'

Kenny's voice was high. 'Don't die!'

'Don't die, Beth!'

'Beth's not going to die, Lily, Kenny, it's all right.'

'But you all want me to. Admit it. It'd all work out if it wasn't for me and my big fat disgusting body.'

'Beth, please, sweetheart.'

'If anyone's going to die any time soon, I think you'll find it'll be me.'

Mum's voice was so small these days, but it cut through us all. I turned so fast to look at her that I screwed the wheel round too, nearly drove onto the pavement. I stamped the brake, and the sudden shock of the stop made Lily cry.

I had thought it'd be all right. I had thought we'd do it, really, we'd been so close.

'Beth, it's not you. It's never you.' And I meant it. Beth was so bright, so pretty. Full of all that rebel energy. It killed me that she had so many friends, attracted all that love, when at home we saw her as the problem.

We were more or less in a lay-by so I turned off the engine. 'I must have done the sums wrong. I don't know. There'll be some way . . . I'll sort it. I'll get another job. Dad, maybe if you, you could . . .' and a big lump came up like I was about to be sick, so I had to stop and swallow before I carried on.

'Oh, I dunno. And Mum, you've got to stop doing this. That so-called Procedure Unit, I'm not going to take you again. I mean they shouldn't be allowed, all that stuff done for money, and they're not even real doctors are they, some of them?'

Mum got hold of my fist that was beating the dashboard. We sat like that for a minute. Kenny reached over the back of my seat and stroked my neck with a little finger. I glanced at him in the mirror. Lily had crawled onto Dad's knee, sniffling into his chest.

I reached round, clawed my fingers. 'What kind of twins are you again?' And I got the instant sunlit squirm from them both.

Behind us all, Beth unsnapped her seatbelt and opened the door into the road.

Shit. I scrambled out and dashed after her. Cars honked and swerved. It was the ring road, for god's sake, slippy already from the new snow. She skipped the crash barrier and stopped as if to check the traffic but she looked down at herself, not at the road. A bus slowed right in front of me and I was faced with a giant Lindt ball being filled with molten caramel, blocking my path.

I got this sort of surge.

I saw exactly what the driver shouted as I ran round. I skidded to the barrier. Beth stepped out into the roadway but I did it, I got her, I grabbed her arm, then I pulled her to me and just hugged and hugged her soft self. We were there a full minute, ten minutes, a lifetime, in the slackening snow, between the oblivious streams of cars. Eventually I felt the buzz of her speaking into my chest. I let her go. Her nose was running. I glanced back at the car, the pale faces of our family.

'Where you going, you big idiot?' I said.

A probationary little smile. '. . . Burger King?'

' _ '

'Joking, duh.' She semi-punched me.

So on Saturday as the streetlights blinked out we were all back in the car, sitting in the same seats but going the other way round the ring road, heading for the A1, everyone jigging about to Jessie J. And I thought about February's money that we'd have to give back and March's money that we wouldn't get, and Special Measures and the twins, how would we, how could we? Unless that other party got in and changed things back, stopped the Formula and re-thought You First, maybe gave everyone a bit of breathing space, I mean there were elections coming, my first time voting, so . . . And I thought about how I'd put our petrol on the credit card again, and that we'd have to pay full admission price which was like forty quid each, no schools' discount, and then there'd be hot dogs and milkshakes and soft toys and branded pencils from the shop, and I thought about how we'd have to sneak Mum onto the Octopus because there was a height minimum. And then I pictured Lily and Kenny screaming happy in the whirly teacups, and Dad reaching for Mum's hand in the café, and me and Beth the spitting image of each other in the gormless photo they take of you at the scariest bit of the Doomacoaster, and us all pointing out the flamingos as if they were a surprise, clue in the name and everything, and so I thought, you know what? I don't care, because no one can force things to be exactly the way they want them to be, not always, maybe not ever.

The Passenger

Katie Willis

A fly followed our mother around because she was born out of wedlock. Damn ugly it was, straight up. Pitch-grey and black with some kind of canker sore on the left wing tip if you put your eyes out for long enough.

Our mother said womenfolk born into estate gardening – where any dot of colour was a murmur of hope – couldn't afford to be finicky. Not when there was no real father about to speak of, at least not one without wings. Not when jewels were missing and no amount of evening primrose planted flat by the south wall could cover up, soft as cream, what was damaged.

It was a recovering woman's need to sleep before the dark came. No matter how fiendishly she worked, how many flower rows she planted. We were born grafters and our mother was recovering from the looks given out down in Jericho Lane. Folk eyeing you in the chest in between blouse buttons, trying to see if the sin of losing one parent made you hollow. Made you a stilt-walker or a freaking runaway.

Neither our mother nor the Passenger (she named the fly on her eighth birthday, marking eight years of acquaintance, after the candles had been blown out but before the cake was cut) were going anywhere.

That was the name to set her free. When life was more than a little throwaway thing. When she got to see the tribulations it put out by standing on the top stair, rising up on tiptoe, her bottom lip pushing out to cover her top, all the time thinking about what it must be like to fly a biplane.

Up there were pride and privacy. The future was sunset. Down on the ground the world was full of hard-as-stone curves that our mother was fond of palpating to yield some air.

When something follows you every which way, you become a lesser version of yourself, a stretch-shadow. And the Passenger was climbing all over our mother's cheek to get the first look in when I was born, coming out lean-to, not quite breech. I did far too much inside dancing when the moonbeams came. I was somewhat of a special case.

Whether our mother was pulling off her skirt or holding a knife handle, she was never alone. In the early years, she worried herself sick but she said that the one thing the Passenger did was take away that niggling concern that she might never have a bed to sleep in with soft white sheets tucked in just so. 'Lays down like a kettle just off the boil. So unbelievable tender,' she said placing it down like a baby on straw, then pushing out her palm like she wanted something put inside it.

I handed her a button from the Spares Box. She seemed bemused, shot it right back. Our mother was all for living out loud with no transgressions. She pulled at a hem thread unravelling. Touched her raggedy hair. 'Hope,' she said. She looked unbelievably wild in the daylight.

It was the Passenger who put the idea in our mother's head that I was infinitely more special than she had ever imagined I could be. It was the Passenger who persuaded her to build a woodshed, hand me over a shovel, a flute and more soft-backed books than I ever found the time to read.

In the autumn of my ninth year, I was whooshed away up a tree in the blast of a west wind. (Our family was flighty.)

The start was there. The second one.

That west wind was downright enchantment. Taught me to take pleasure in the smallest things when I was halfway up a beechwood tree in striped culottes. My top was torn, once at the hem and again at the cuff. I wasn't the smartest of girls but I was courting no ghost company. I had plans. None of them involved children.

'Generation begets generation,' I whispered. Nothing was ever truly broken, that much I knew. But the chinks were there. Right from the start. With my legs dangling from a beechwood bough (they were scratched all over from spending time reading for pleasure in the bushes), I prayed out to the sweetest god (whom I had grown in an old Coke bottle, circa 1950s). I had him there beside me like an extra limb. I was never spiteful. Not the way hornets are. The venom I inherited came from my father's side, and I squashed it deep to form a tube, made a hole in it like velvet.

I sat up straight in quiet celebration. Who said you couldn't start making your own world when you sure as hell felt like it?

'Tell me when you were born.' I knew that voice. Suss. Suss. It came with the Passenger. Came that time with sunset and a push-out treacle sky.

Our mother was always asking questions. She said that growth came from unexpected places, from answering any which way with the exception of a pernickety tone.

'Ten past three in the morning. Day before Easter. When the coast was clear.'

'Good. God bless us one and all,' she said, the Passenger hovering about her right ear.

Three Amens stopped her hacking away at it. She took out the comb she always carried in her apron pocket. Eliminated kinks. Eliminated frizz. When she did those things, I knew she was saved. Knew she was becoming a normal woman standing masterful beneath a beechwood tree.

She was shining but there were cobwebs on the hem of her gingham dress. She wasn't the smartest dresser either. It was a family thing. It travelled down the female line. She looked out bug-eyed towards the Crook Valley, propped up her head with her hands.

There were some places our mother went just

to be alone. Places where she was missing, where she sold out. Crook Valley was one of them. But I knew that all she needed was holding down for long enough so she had the chance to quiet down, start over.

Start over. That made for a third beginning.

My god was encased in glass. Just as well. Just as well. Nothing better than to encapsulate the best. I wasn't quite flying, but I was close enough and feeling safe rocking my legs, making up songs about having a good life.

A moment frozen right there. I was singing my guts out and our mother was breaking through the mist, tender-hearted. Together we were strong. So strong . . .

My god was no good when the stick man came barefoot out of the coppice, stumbling not walking. No trousers, just old faded-from-washing pants, a belt when there was nothing to push it through, and legs streaked the colour of bindweed. My god was busy working, working to save all the children in the world, beating back the past so I could be born again. My god had no eyes for the half-light of the night. He never saw ugly stick man crazy from marching out with a burnt ring finger.

I did.

What kind of pain was it that made a man lick his finger gentle, so tender, the way you lick the cream from the top of a trifle?

That was a soft, sweet path the stick man took with his eyes puffed out. And you'd come the sweetest way too if you were hell-bent on destruction. Not too shrill. Not too powerful. Resetting your step, glazing over rationality, greasing the lock. Clever. Oh so clever.

Suss. Suss. There was the Passenger again. Our mother tapped repeatedly at her head. And then she started whispering about diminishing and how she had no one to blame.

No one. Not yet. Those were my god's words when he woke up. They came through me flawless like the sun on a hot day. And that was when I knew the stick man's finger was burned only because he wanted it that way, staring out at an open flame, peeling himself apart, enraged, the victim he thought himself to be smouldering away inside. I shivered even though there was no chill to the day. I tucked in my chin.

'Ain't so much this side of the river,' stick man said dabbing at rolling sweat with a filthy handkerchief, parting his lips to show off gaps and black where solid teeth should sit. 'Except perhaps a part-pretty lady and a damn scrap girl. Beauty in that.' He slapped at his pants. Undid his belt.

I was more than damn scrap. Much more. But I was not charmed and that was my downfall.

I heard stick man say that our mother's part-prettiness kicked in big time from the waist down. What with some kind of luxury material and the way it push-poked like it wanted to fly. I heard him laugh, a cut-glass laugh that stopped just short of his chest, and I raised my head a little but I couldn't get interested in being part of his world.

Out of the corner of my eye, I saw the hem of our mother's luxury gingham go up when there was no wind to push it. Someone hit the ground. Someone rolled about amongst crackle leaves. Someone was scrambling. Someone was crying the way wolves do when the hunger kneads at them in the unlit night, reduces them to bones.

There was a slap. And another. There was gasping and panting. More crying. There was rutting and the sound of cotton being stripped apart and my god was all for noticing things then and he didn't like it. Told me to fix my eyes on an abandoned house that had once been oh-so-pretty popping up over the hill. And so I did, singing love songs smooth as butter to the half-missing roof and fallen structural beams.

Sometimes when you can't bear what you see you become a bird in panic bouncing off the walls. Where is the string to make a net to keep your heart complete?

I was crying the way you do when a coffin's lowered into the ground and you know the person inside it.

I came back with a jolt from the empty house with the swing-off-its-hinges door to hear our mother sobbing down amongst the leaves where the world had no name. Scrubbing my face dry, I heard her say in a high-pitched voice that she had such despair as to rip her spleen out from inside but I wasn't to worry. Oh no. For worry was a rent when things were better fine. And I was to note that she was only rubbing the small of her back to push in what had been robbed from her, to get the juices flowing.

'Quicksilver juices,' she whispered clutching at the top of her legs. Her voice was four hills and a valley. She was all fired up. I thought I saw the start of it.

'Are you really in flames?' I shouted looking around for stick man. He was nowhere to be seen. Some kind of soft wind had ripped him free.

Our mother swallowed twice to prepare for the answer. Looked back at the top part of her legs. 'Some kind of glue, so sticky,' she screamed and she looked like she did when she'd worked too long with a fork on the flower border, mournful inside.

'Wanting so bad to soak my skin,' she whispered turning begging eyes at me, her fingers pushing rough on her thighs. I gave her what I had. Soft eyes. It was a love exchange. She felt it. I knew she did.

Then something changed and it was scalping a man alive when all our mother needed was hugging to force the evil out. It was that kind of agony.

'The Passenger!' our mother screamed, tapping at her head, tapping at her collarbone, banging at her chest. 'Where in God's name?' She put a thumb between her legs. Could she really find it that way? Reach somewhere deep inside?

The Passenger was dead. It was slurry over by her left foot, its wings clipped of flight. 'And that's put paid to ancestry,' our mother spluttered seeing it gone. She was half-crying then, making quiet sounds insufficient to bring it back. She tugged at her hair. I'd seen her do that with weeds so the best things could grow free.

'When I'm done for, make sure you bury me with my head pointing north,' our mother said. She cooed like a dove bird, plucked at feathers she did not have. Where did that come from? She was a naked child then and life was shameful. Four minutes, maybe five and her hands were shaking from over-plucking. She clenched one, yanked one back.

'It's important. Promise.' She was pleading with me, not with her hands but with her head, raising it the way chickens do when they're spooked.

I was broken inside jumping down from the beechwood. I put my god down amongst the leaves and went for the clenched hand first, ironed it out flat, planted kisses on the fingertips, one, two, three, four, five. 'Hang by me,' I said. I was mollifying. I pulled the gingham straight like only a girl can do, brushed at the waist so it laid flat. I was remembering, not looking back. Life rolled over. Dead. With two of us broken.

We began again.

The fourth start.

Because of the break inside, I was ready to pitch and run as fast as my legs could carry me but my god was clamouring hard for me to stay.

Be a woman.

But I'm just a girl.

Steady now. Be tall as a redwood.
I'm only four foot nine.
You are impenetrable.
I am nothing of the kind.

Our mother broke away from me and spoke about laundry. About how taking it in could be her new life calling. Turning just the one hand into a clothes brush, she scrubbed away at all the stains she could find. 'Nice company for the sun,' she said, transforming the brush into a clothesline, stepping up on wood to peg the washing tight. 'Make room for the sheets, remember,' she whispered, and there were tears on her cheeks as she pretended to wander back indoors, the sky still blue with the sun gone in.

There were spores of daisies growing in her outside world. It was the hold of something fresh and sweet and I got that right from the start bending down to pick up my god.

Then our mother was sobbing. She was back on her hands and knees like the family rabbit looking for pretty, real pretty. 'Where in God's name is it?' she screamed rocking north to south, north to south, holding on to her belly, patching up things that needed patching. She felt for her throat and vomited up her lunch food.

It set my teeth on edge. I turned away. Could I beat up a man?

Could I wrap a rope down his spine, bone on bone, and pull?

I was tight to our mother then, wiping away tears, giving what I could.

Never go alone into the clearing. The foxes get to you that way.

Our mother pushed away from me, bent across and scooped up the Passenger. Held it to her breast like she used to hold me. 'My baby ain't happy,' she said flexing her feet and stroking a wing. That was the first time I'd heard her call it that and I thought she'd forgotten that it was gone. She was moving away with it so still. Looking for some kind of focus.

'Did you kill it?' she asked. Her eyes were dry, the whites of them fading.

'No,' I said. There was no darkness in my reply but our mother found some anyway. Told me off for speaking in an over-whiny voice.

She mentioned burial. Said the Passenger should go back to its maker.

My god spoke out then as I planted my ankles in leaves.

We are not ready.

But our mother needs this. She needs something to end right.

Wait awhile for a sign.

How long must we wait?

Until the moon comes up.

We were not waiting. Not waiting for the moon. Not waiting for anyone. And if I went behind my god's back, who could blame me? I was no sneak. I had a clear purpose. I was pulling our mother with one hand.

Pulling her – a horse-on-wheels with one of the wheels gone.

'No trousers,' our mother spluttered, holding the Passenger under her chin like it was a daisy telling her if she was loved or not. She was bereft. Squinting like her face was pulped, teasing her hair like she was smashing a way out, she made a slow cross sign on her left thigh. 'What kind of decent person walks out with no trousers on?'

I stroked her hand to stop the blood coming from her bit lip and I thought about what people did when the floods came. Did they make it out alive?

Four steps into the clearing and our mother collapsed like the air had been taken out of her. 'Loves you, loves you not, loves you plenty in death,' I whispered, looking up at the Passenger soft-dead in her hand.

I heard her humming away to beat back the past. *Hmm la hmm la la. Hmm la hmm la la. La. La.* She stopped too soon. Before her world had quietened down.

'Pretty tune,' I whispered, bending to kiss her on the nose, just above the bloody lip. She reeled. Stumbled back in time. She didn't have a clue how to take that glut of love. So I pulled some back. Made like the road ahead was straight and governable.

'Can anyone read minds?' she asked. Her eyes were shining like the sun poking through.

'Anyone?'

'Mostly you,' she said.

'No.' I was definite with that. My god was not

for mind-reading, only acts of kindness. That's the difference between dry land and being out at sea.

Say it. Say it. Say it. That was what my god demanded. So together we said a prayer for the dead. I was just a girl praying, each word a splinter in glass.

Put out kind words.

I did not. I wrapped a rope around ugly stick man's spine to end him there. Snap. Once before the Amen. Snap again after. And he didn't even fight. Just screamed the once, pushed his belly out.

Ugly fool, I thought. And Jesus, he was tiny. Just skin on stick-out bones, his bindweed legs smudged nonsensical. 'Rest with pigs,' I mocked. Nine years on this earth and I was as tall as a poplar tree. I could kill the way soldiers did.

No. No. That's not the way, my god said.

It was the perfect way.

I leaned down, retied my shoe, little by little realising that the bright in our mother's eyes was nothing but a dead vacancy when sorrow was buried too deep to surface.

We never made it home straight off. For starters our mother was all bent up. She was tattle twist. Crooked in places that were never meant to shift. Turning, turning her hand on her skirt, she was a spider trapped in a web. But you couldn't take the rage out of gingham. You just went on doing what you were doing until the madness stopped.

Our mother sent back her neck to recover some of what was lost. She was quite far gone.

'Show me the way,' she said. And I pointed my god north through the line of trees to the clearing beyond. 'Who will announce our return?' she asked.

There was no one to do that.

'Weeell,' our mother screamed, 'then tonight let's have oyster mushrooms.' She was tripping a step, licking her index finger and pushing it out into the wind. Lifting the Passenger high, she put it in a place where it could love anything it chose. And her cheeks were shimmering wet when shimmer was a storm in waiting. When the soft moan that came from her throat made me want to pull on a wishbone and dream.

I was all eyes on our mother's back as she pushed along despairing, forced her heels into the earth she hoped would take her home. 'As you said you wanted it all along,' she whispered, looking up to address the Passenger. From where I was, it seemed like angels were coming. Our mother was so crooked and strong, her hair flying out at all angles, matted on the right side, making a house for birds to nest in. Was she broken at the roots?

Instinctively I reached out. There was nothing more beautiful than the way that I loved her, risking everything for some kind of shine that would serve as a miraculous resurrection.

Not all things can be fixed, my god whispered.

Something inside that had been coiled in such a soft place, came up. Made me not murderous (I had done enough killing already) but fierce through to the bone.

The sun came out right when the night was starting. Broke soft through pewter. I wanted to say something. Anything. But I couldn't form the words. So I opened the bottle. Turned it upside down. Made a way out.

I set someone free.

Purple Haze

Sanya Semakula

When Uncle Mgapi dies it will split up the family.
That's why he holds on, lying there in that hospital
bed with his flesh clinging to his limbs and every
wheeze of breath pushing through stifled lungs. I
want him to let go.

Abu takes me to see him two days before he
passes away. Abu is seventeen and lives with Uncle
Mgapi. Since his mum moved to Huntingdon he has
started selling so that he can save a bit for himself.
He has a 20-bag but no grinder. I have to pick the
weed and the smell soaks into my hands.

We smoke outside a block of council flats not
too far away from Newham General Hospital.
When Abu gets high he laughs at everything. *Man,
look how far the sky is,* he giggles. *Mean . . . how
the fuck do we get planes up there?*

Weed always makes me feel breakable. My
collarbone is out of place, straining against my
flesh. When I walk, my kneecaps try to dislocate as
if the rest of me will come sliding through. The
worst thing is that I say things I never knew I felt:

When Uncle dies I'll be an orphan.

Your mumsy is still alive. Edjiot. Bet you dun know what the word means. Abu laughs. *These trees are orphans though.*

What the fuck are you talking about? I screw up my face.

Man's high, innit? Purple Haze. Buzzzzzing. He leans his head back and chuckles, high cheekbones spiking up and white teeth against night-black skin.

Will you have to move out then? I ask Abu. *I mean, with your mum and that?*

Abu squints, with his face tilted towards the sky as if he is searching for the answer in the clouds. His nostrils expand as his mouth tightens around the roach. His index finger and thumb press down as the joint burns to its final toke.

Big man will make it through . . . trust me. His sentence comes through smoke and strained lungs.

Man like me knows this, Uncle Mgapi has been a warrior since day . . . Let's go.

When we get to Uncle Mgapi's room it smells like laundry and bad breath. The white walls keep closing in and every once in a while transform into a face. Angry. Smiling. Winking. My vision blurs as everything spins into that familiar swirl.

This has happened once before. I'm about to pull a whitey.

Calm down little cuz, calm yourself. It's cool. He's asleep.

I can't breathe man, Abs. I can't breathe. I need to get out please, I whisper back to Abu. We leave. We don't say goodbye, no kisses on the cheek, no pat on the hands. We leave him still sleeping. I puke in the parking lot.

We are not allowed to speak about Uncle Mgapi — not after he is dead. The subjects of our conversations are reserved for the living and my family knows that the best way to deal with grief is to keep it bottled up until it shrivels to a size that you can ignore.

We are allowed to cry but only at the funeral. There you're allowed to beat your chest, curse your mother, roll around the floor and pull your hair out. At the wake you're allowed to eat your energy back with all the food but know that that first bite signals the end of your sorrow.

Abu comes to the funeral service late and you can smell the weed straight away. He is in an oversized black suit that hangs from his lanky frame like sagging skin. Uncle Mgapi gave this to him for his first job interview. The pants are tied in tight with a leather belt and he is wearing his black Puma trainers.

He stands at the entrance of the church as if he is unsure whether he'll stay. When he sits down there is a smirk at the edges of his mouth and tears are running down his face. He sits right behind my mum, Najja.

Najja is a time bomb waiting to blow. Sat at the front, she keeps rocking in her seat; her black-and-green Gomesi makes ruffled noises as she goes back and forth, whispering *Mukama.*

Mukama. Mukama. Mukama. The chant starts dancing in my head. *God. God. God.* I repeat in rhythm with her and hope whoever she is praying to will give her comfort. She keeps on looking to the coffin as if at any moment her brother will jump up and end this practical joke.

Uncle Mgapi wanted to be buried in Uganda but when you're dead your wishes go with you. It's an open casket and he looks like an ash-black mannequin. Najja grasps his limp arms and for a moment as she pulls they look like they'll come out of their sockets.

She grabs on to the coffin and wails as if her screams will wake him back to life. Two burly men have to wrestle her away. They're some kind of relatives but they're not her brother and so she hits out, spits and cries all at once. She's a large woman, she uses her body weight against the men and wiggles free.

Why him? God, why him? She shouts at the rest of us, looking wildly from face to face as if ready to make a bargain: anyone else for him. Any one.

Tonight I get high. I jump over our back garden fence into Ashburton Wood. I sit on a stone and blow smoke to the trees. I finish a 10-bag – two spliffs – and melt into the stone below.

I'm made of solid mass and rooted in the ground. Worms slither and insects crawl about beneath me. Whole communities of families lost in wordless conversations: they'll bicker, make love, and gossip about the warmth of my skin.

It's the moon that brings me back into my flesh. It whistles with the wind and holds itself steady in the waves of the night. The pace of the wind slows down as it runs through my hair. I want to stay here all night but there is something unpleasant about the way the light falls through the trees, going between the leaves and tracing its way down their trunks. There is movement in their stillness, slight and subtle enough to fool the eyes, but I feel them dragging towards me, and my vision is starting to blur.

I climb the fence and land unsteady on the ground. The earth slides below me and my ankles are out of place as if my shoes are on the wrong feet. All that sitting down has bent my spine to the side of my stomach and my ribs push against my skin as if looking for an exit.

I feel my hand close around the back-door handle. My knuckles feel like they have slid to my fingertips and everything is hard to grip.

I can hear the woods behind me and the neighbours whispering in my ears. I know that they're all watching, waiting to see what will happen but I have to listen out for Najja. If I wake her up she'll see the red around my eyes and think that I've been crying.

The door creaks open. My trainers are in my hands. The carpet rises between my toes. My head feels too heavy for my neck. The weight pulls me to my knees. I'm crawling to my bedroom. The carpet is maroon. I'm thinking of the Red Sea and I'm thinking I'm Moses. I'm not sure who I'm supposed to set free but I'm sure I'll let them down. Besides, I hate burning bushes.

Another whitey.

Abu taught me how to deal with these. He said you're supposed to smoke right through them but I can't move. Not like that. Not upright.

I pull my knees to my chest. My heart and brain have swapped places. My heart is in my head; it drums a beat in my ears. I wish it would stop.

I dream of Uncle Mgapi. He is walking through Rathbone Market. I'm standing outside the library across the road but I can see him clearly. He goes from stall to stall asking for something but the people shake their heads. When he sees me he rushes over. He talks but there is no sound. I can't understand him. He grabs my shoulders and shakes me but I don't know what he wants.

Abu is twenty and he has moved from selling weed to money transfers. It's a business that I don't understand but there is a group of boys who have to listen to what he says – he is middle management.

He has a rented room in a house in Dagenham and I visit him in secret. After our mums fell out we all had to pick sides. Someone mentioned Uncle Mgapi but no one really knows how the fight started. Sera got drunk and said something about

AIDS. We never speak about AIDS. We've put it in that bottle – we're waiting for it to shrivel to a size we can ignore.

I like Sera. She isn't like her sister, my mum. She is free-spirited and she says what she feels. She comes to church in tight black jeans and killer heels with her hair in an afro like a black halo. She flirts with visiting pastors and men half her age. She talks about her sex life at family gatherings. She isn't a good Ugandan woman. Najja says she's been too Westernised but I think she's always had this streak.

I tease Abu about his latest girlfriend as he crushes the crystals with a credit card.

I only date white girls cos they're easier. Trust me, black girls have too much lip, he tells me. I think he just doesn't want to date anyone who would remind him of his mum but I say nothing.

He rubs the two balls in his hands and gives me one. They're made out of rolling paper and twisted at the top. You could mistake them for sweets.

How old are you again?

Seventeen, you douchebag.

I'm definitely going to hell, Abu laughs. He throws the ball in the air; he tilts his head and catches it in his mouth. I wash mine down with water. It's bitter. Like medicine but worse. I copy Abu and slide a finger in the crushed dust on the edges of the credit card. I run it along my gums and try not to pull a face.

The come-up is . . . a head rush. In a second,

reality strips naked and bends herself out of form.

The room begins to dance, wobbling out of shape. Abu is lying shirtless on his bed. His bed is a sea of navy blue and he keeps sinking into the waves. He lifts his right arm up and twists his fingers, playing with the light that bounces off his palm.

I'm sat by the computer with my leg jumping up and down. The world is running through my calves, whole landscapes formed in my tendons. I feel a wind climbing up inside my back, blowing the leaves hanging from my spine. There are birds tweeting just behind my jaw. *Let's go out*, I tell Abu and we go out to fly.

From Dagenham to Custom House we fly through clouds that change shapes. Most of the people down below don't notice us, only a few look up. They all have blurred faces and it's hard to make out their features.

We land in the Greenway leading to Beckton. The ground is made of elastic. Bushes stick out branched arms for high fives. One tugs at my jogging bottoms trying to pull me into itself but I wiggle away. We stop by a pond made entirely of green liquorice and I say: *This is the greenest of the greens.*

We sit on a bench. It rubs itself up and down our thighs trying to seduce us to stay. I make up a poem:

The trees so high up never look down below for us, so we might as well chop wood.

Neither of us understands it. It makes no sense but Abu begs me to repeat it and taps it into his phone. When we get back to Abu's house I'm still restless. I spin around his tiny room. My arms detach and fly about like kites and I can't remember where I left my toes.

Abu plays Leadbelly, 'Good Morning Blues'. The riff comes in and runs its fingers down my face and digs its nails across my neck.

Oh Lord, I was turning from side to side. I wasn't sad, I was just dissatisfied, Leadbelly sings. My pelvis jolts out of place and his voice rolls me into a ball, pushing my chest against my thighs. I want to say something like: *What is it about the blues that punches you in the gut of your soul?* but instead I say: *Did you know Mgapi means 'pillar of the community'?*

We're not allowed to talk about Uncle Mgapi. Abu keeps quiet. I change the subject. He makes two more balls of crystal and this time we stay in, floating somewhere near his ceiling.

When we come down I get up to leave. It's late. Abu walks me to the door. *Tomorrow you'll feel like shit*, he says, but he already looks it. He hands me a 10-bag and we stand in his doorway. He looks like he could break. Like when I leave he'll spill over, melting to the ground, and when I come to look for him he'll just be a black substance on the floor, in the corner of the room.

The day I leave for university Abu comes over to help me pack. His new job has its risks: there is a scar in the middle of his left eyebrow where hair has refused to grow back. He has moved from money transfers to class As and although he has youngas – musclemen – he still gets caught in street fights.

This your big send-off, little cuz. Abu smiles, readjusting himself on the edge of my bed. He unzips his black Just-Do-It Nike backpack and looks around.

What, you giving me Pees? I laugh.

Not even, student finance got you with that one. Abu pulls out a big silver wallet, tin foil and Blu Tack from his bag. *Pass me that.* He points to an empty 500ml Coca-Cola bottle.

He makes a bong. Stabs two holes in the bottle, one three-quarters of the way up and the other close to the lid. He gets a biro and takes off both ends, removing the inside part so that we can make the outside into a tube. He puts the tube through the lower hole so one end touches the bottom of the bottle and the other sticks out of the hole. He makes a cone-shaped bowl out of tin foil and puts the green tobacco-like substance into it. Abu then sticks the tin foil around the mouth of the tube and holds it together with Blu Tack. *Makes it airtight, innit?* he smiles.

What's this? I ask as Abu fills the bottle halfway up with water.

Salvia bruv – and popo can't say nothing cos it's legal.

It looks like weed.

Yeah but it screws you up differently, Abu laughs, handing me the bong.

I take a hit. My lips cover the mouth of the bottle. I put my thumb over the hole at the top just as Abu taught me. The smoke builds up with the boiling water and I remove my thumb and inhale.

My room slides out of focus, cream walls replaced with a vacant darkness. Then I'm transported: I am at sea. I am a lifeboat. I am rubber pumped up with air. My engine is my heart; my heart is strong. My skin slaps the water. The tides are high but I am a lifeboat.

There is wailing in the air, a screech that bangs hard against your eardrums. There are other people here too, but they are not people. They're rafts, canoes and big ships that blow black air into the blue sky. We're all going the same way. We're all running from the same thing.

I turn around and spot Sera. She is a flimsy raft. Her planks are held together with seaweed and she is slowly falling apart as the tides crush against her. I look beyond her. Far off, just a spot in the distance is what we all fear. It's where the scream is coming from. I squint to see.

There is a person – a real person. His arms wave frantically through the air as he tries to keep his head above the waters. I'm trying to work out who it is, straining to see – that's when my engine skips a beat. The guy . . . the guy is Abu.

The phone call comes in my last term at university. I haven't spoken to Abu or his mum in two years but I heard Sera married and moved to America.

You should come visit me, Sera chuckles on the phone. *You'd love Rob and his kids and I'll take you out to L.A.* We speak for an hour and every minute I can sense that she is gearing herself up to roll the conversation to the point of the call.

Have you spoken to your mum lately? Her voice sounds nervous.

Not really. What's up with Najja? I ask.

Najja had quickly found a way to deal with her grief like women who keep cats she started collecting books to fill a void. There were books leaning against every wall of her house except in the kitchen. She bought books in languages that she couldn't read, bought the same book twice if it had a different cover . . . but her speciality was Bibles. Bibles of every size; big, small, slim, all in different languages, as if she was trying to cram God into her little house and this time get Him to listen.

Do you think you can call her? If you're not busy, I mean, Sera asks. We change the subject. She tells me about the weather where she lives and about her new diet.

When we get off the phone I try to remember Uncle Mgapi. He was tall, so tall that he had to bend through doorways. His shoulders were wide and he had those back dimples between each blade, that dent that men get when they exercise too much.

He was full of muscles from hard labour. He worked at the Sunny Delight factory, long hours that would see him crawl back home with the moon and crawl back out again while it still lingered in the sky. He was a soft-spoken man with a deep voice that seemed incapable of rising in volume no matter how angry he got. He never had any kids but when Sera moved to Huntingdon with her boyfriend, he took Abu in. I remember that I never cried for Uncle Mgapi.

I dial Najja's number as I recall all of this. The last time we spoke was when I left for university. I'm trying to think of an excuse for calling when someone picks up. She tells me she's a family friend. She tells me that Najja is not in.

Any idea when I should call back? I ask. There is silence. I try again in broken Luganda.

When she finally figures out what I'm trying to say the woman replies: *Well, she's gone to see Abu so I can't be sure.* I ask her to explain.

Yagudde edalu.

He has fallen ill? No. He has fallen into sickness? No. He has fallen into madness? Almost. I ask her to explain again.

He lost his mind. When his mum left. It slipped out of his nose. He smoked too much. Got baked and burnt everything inside. He thought it would cool off in the snow. Went looking for something that morning. Cold winter. He walked from Dagenham to Custom House and all the way through the Greenway. He walked through Canning Town and crossed the bridge to the Docklands.

He circled around West India Quay and went back to the Docklands. The police found him in Beckton District Park. They took him to Newham General Hospital. A boy black like night walking around like that in the snow was bound to cause alarm. He had no shoes on his feet and when he found his perfect spot he stripped down, bollock naked, and spoke to the trees.

I'm thinking of the last time I spoke to Abu when I come off the phone. He called me late one night. London filtered through the phone line and our voices struggled to be heard between the sirens and the car sounds. Before we said goodbye, Abu asked why I went so far away and then laughed and said he understood, though I hadn't given him an answer.

I go to the corner shop and buy two bottles of red wine. The best way to handle grief is to let it shrivel to a size you can ignore.

Mrs Świętokrzyskie's Castle

Colette Sensier

Mrs Świętokrzyskie calls Josef. He says he's working, too busy to talk, but she'd swear she can hear the latest girl kissing the back of his neck. 'Josef, today I think I will go out.'

'OK, Ma.'

'You want to come with me? You can bring Kristen, if you would like to.'

'Mum . . .' His voice drops. 'It's Ilana, you know that.' Blaming her perfectly good memory for his loose living.

'You want to bring Ilana? That's fine.'

'Actually, Mum, it's a bit of a tricky day for me . . .' He laughs. 'Where you going, anyway?'

'First, I will go to Buckingham Palace. We could have tea in the park.'

Josef laughs again, louder. Mrs Świętokrzyskie's children have been in England too long and they never want to go anywhere: spoilt. Herself, she likes to sit in the fine green park by the palace, half tourist and half proprietor. After being disappointed, early on, by Tower Hill, this is now her model of the perfect castle: the symmetry, the gold, the guards, the many gates.

She wishes she could build this palace; but she'd add dragons. And flying monkeys clutching daggers, instead of guards.

Lords and ladies, she imagines from their confident walks, go past her in plain suits and low heels. She sits on the bench with her Thermos and sandwiches in Tupperware until she gets too cold. Pulls her imaginary fur up around her. She never sees fur in this country; except the white mink cape which flows over her shoulders, framing her metal-plated breasts.

Mrs Świętokrzyskie lives in a basement flat, in a block the council made in the sixties by squashing three manor houses into one. If you stood in the alley beside the block, you could touch her living-room window. Because of the angle of the window-frame, you'd only see an old lady's head of hair, white highlighted with iron grey, and below it her big green armchair – the kind that passes through a cycle of empires and emigrations, fashions and wars before landing up in flats like this, gilt feet flaking, stuffing thin. You'd see Mrs Świętokrzyskie's long dark skirt and bright loose-fitting T-shirt, and the white hair highlighted with iron grey.

You'd think perhaps the old lady was reading, or sewing, or looking over old photos or letters. Perhaps you'd feel sad for her, that she only has one low-energy bulb to see by, the pink-shaded lamp holding her in a rosy circle. The thought might even cross your mind — considering old people, foreign people, living alone in a big careless city — that she is dead, has died, and that's why she's slumped in her chair so late at night, so still.

But look again at her hands. Not the wrinkles like scrunched-up silk or the puckered skin round the wrists, but the position of her hands — the wrists dip low, moving fast as dancers across the keyboard of the computer on her desk.

Just outside your view, the light hidden inside the computer buckles and hisses. Mrs Świętokrzyskie thinks of the landfill she saved the computer from when Josef's office chucked it out. She thinks of the poor thing lying alone and dead, spreading its poisonous roots into the ground — irradiating the soil probably, burning the young bulbs. She's saved the computer, and she's protected the world from it.

Her eagle-winged, cat-suited avatar clutches two top-range crossbows in each hand.

READY?

Mrs Świętokrzyskie has a secret. She has met a man.

Bernard came out of nowhere to challenge her a few months ago. She's a few levels ahead of him, but not many, hardly enough to matter: three. His avatar is a blue dragon with a long neck and protruding eyes, ungainly as a giraffe, skin like old leather. The dragon wears silver chain-mail armour trimmed with red-and-white fur.

The two of them drew their swords and struggled for a good twenty minutes, Bernard displaying an impressive stockpile of Revivors. But Mrs Świętokrzyskie had bought a magic apple from a witch in Round 23, and when she was on the ground, about to choke, the apple sucked out the last of Bernard's strength and bestowed it on her.

Fair fight: the letters appeared one by one in the speech bubble.

Mrs Świętokrzyskie didn't know exactly what he meant by 'fair'. Was he being sarcastic, implying that the use of the apple – as opposed to his more modest Revivors – was cheating? Or did he mean 'fair play', 'fair enough'? Was he congratulating her?

She took a risk and typed out: *Thank You.*

The next day she woke up annoyingly early, 7 a.m. The shifts at the hospital ruin her sleep pattern; sometimes she'll sleep fourteen hours, or crash in the middle of the day. Now she wasn't due at work for another eleven hours. She tried to read in bed but couldn't. She dared herself not to turn on the computer yet, and instead had a long bath with lavender extract, ate two bowls of cereal.

She got dressed – right up to tights and jewellery – before calling her daughter. Around eleven was a good time to call, but when Gabriela answered today she sounded a little flustered. 'Gabriela, if you have the babies with you, it's no trouble, I can go.'

'No Ma, it's fine, Ryan's at school . . . it's just that it's not Magda's nursery day today and she's got a friend over, so I really should be watching them.' Her heeled shoes clicked across linoleum at the other end of the country. 'There – they're in the living room. I can see them from here.'

'And is it a good day? Is the weather good, up in Glasgow?'

'It's good, Ma.'

Mrs Świętokrzyskie thought Gabriela was not really listening to her, laughing to herself – not very polite. She gripped the receiver firmly. They took up a lot of her time, these phone calls. She was a busy woman with her job, her walks, her son, but she didn't begrudge Gabriela the time.

'It's really good.' Gabriela paused. 'You know, Ma, I worry about you down there on your own. Is it true Josef's moved out for good?'

'Oh, your brother has had his own flat for years now.'

'You know what I mean, Ma . . . Well, I suppose he must nip back to get his shirts ironed every once in a while.'

Mrs Świętokrzyskie thought she could hear her granddaughter in the background. Ela's house was always full of noise.

'You'd like it up here you know, Ma. There's plenty of Polish families, and the neighbours are all so friendly. Not like the old place at all. You know, you walk out the door here and the people next door know my name, they know Magda's name . . . It's nice.'

'Yes, Ela, lovely. Do you know, I saw that woman

in the hallway today and she doesn't say a word to me? Not even good morning? And she's been here, what, six months, since last October – no, must be seven . . .'

'The Iranian one?'

'No, Gabriela! That was Mrs Far, Mrs Fah something – she's been gone now a good year – ten months at least. Well, she wasn't here at Easter, was she?'

'I don't know, Ma.' The *Ma* has happened since Gabriela moved to Scotland, she'd always called Mrs Świętokrzyskie *Mum*, growing up.

'You must remember if you saw her at Easter! That's the last time you were down here . . .'

'Look Ma, I've got to go. You should come up, you know, if you're lonely. The kids would love to see more of you . . . And Jamie wouldn't mind.'

But Mrs Świętokrzyskie has moved once already, across the whole of Europe. She doesn't intend to move again. Here she has Josef; she has a new girlfriend of Josef's to meet every few months; she has her girls at her hospital, and she has a Silver Sword ranking on the computer.

She lit a cigarette and sat down at her desk, the sharp brooch on her jumper prickling her chin. The computer makes a fearful noise – though with Josef's tinkering, and the little black box he's given her, it copes quite well. She imagined it straining to reach MagiKingdom like a pigeon might strain with a crucial ten-page letter strapped to its back.

She loaded her account up with money and

bought two outfits, a new MasterSword, and a blue peacock for her castle – and in her inbox was a Private Message from the blue dragon.

That was six months ago. Now, she duels with Bernard two or three times a week. In between, he emails her. His hours are more regular than hers: he gets home at six o'clock on the dot, every day, and usually she has an email by seven.

With no degree and shaky written English, Mrs Świętokrzyskie is not a nurse. She is a healthcare assistant, and she feeds the patients and removes their waste, turns and washes their big bodies all day. So whatever time she comes home, the first thing she does is take off her shoes.

As she sits in her big green armchair, she reaches down to rub her sore feet in between the levels on the games. She lights a cigarette. A message is in.

> Klara,
> Just got in from the Office, wondering how you're day went?! hope to chat to you later, and that girl Abby hasn't been giving you grief. Today we had a complaint so I was 'on the phone' all day! But it'll make my day better to see you later on around the Marketplace. All my Best,
> B

He's a good man. He's a kind, good man, and his emails are something to hold on to. And he knows what it's like to lose a child; although his daughter is only in Australia. She's his only one, and he knows what it's like to miss, twenty years too late, the warm heft of a child's body in your lap. Mrs Świętokrzyskie can talk to him about Władysława, about the long years when she wasn't here and they didn't know if she was anywhere else; and about the phone call telling her that her daughter was dead, in such a horrible way, and about how nothing has ever seemed truly normal since.

Bernard must be very lonely, because when Mrs Świętokrzyskie gets back from a fifteen-hour shift one day in June, she finds three emails waiting for her. She answers them all at once, and then they both log on to MagiKingdom, where together they slay a witch in disguise and take from her two PowerSwords, a Vengeance Potion, and seven frogs' legs, which aren't worth much.

Bernard bought her the first leopard.

About three months ago the gawky blue dragon approached her in the forest, and in his hand was a lead attached to the collar of a beautiful, slow-moving cat. Its eyes were blue like sapphires, the pixels of its fur smooth and bright. As Mrs Świętokrzyskie admired it, the animal suddenly swelled to fill her whole screen. A message flashed up:

ITEM: Roaming Leopard.
CATEGORY: Guard Animal.
STRENGTH: Eight.
FLEXIBILITY: Nine.
SURVIVAL CAPACITY: Six.
COST: $40.

ACCEPT GIFT?

The leopard's figure revolved, shadowed into 3-D, and it moved its head a little and twitched its tail.

YES, she clicked.

She hasn't told anyone about Bernard, but their interaction is written plain on the computer for anyone to see who cares to look. She doesn't hide his emails; she flaunts his leopard at the head of her pack.

Now she has fifty leopards, all except Bernard's gift bought and paid for by herself. It doesn't do to depend on men: that's why she's always kept her job. She'd had to retrain in England, but it was worth it, because now she can provide for herself.

Six months doesn't seem like a long time to Mrs Świętokrzyskie. Time flies by so quickly as you get older or when you're getting that way. Up in Scotland, Gabriela's pregnant again. Mrs Świętokrzyskie doesn't know how much Ela wants all these babies. She's used to seeing her daughter being the eldest, bossing younger children around, and this doesn't seem much of a change. How can Gabriela tell if she wants to live this life, when it so closely resembles her old one? Even her little flat in Glasgow could almost be Mrs Świętokrzyskie's.

Meanwhile the castle has grown and grown. She doesn't have to worry about money, with her salary, Jan's life insurance, and a mortgage paid off as soon as possible after they bought the flat from the council in 1983. She's been spending it on turrets, and gilt chandeliers and tableware, and her own personalised coat of arms.

Her castle has a drawbridge with a moat, and she doesn't often let the drawbridge down. She likes knowing it's there. The castle has a turret at each corner, with walkways running between them. The walkways are protected by walls with arrow-holes cut in them, so that her archers can crouch down and shoot at invaders from a safe height.

Mrs Świętokrzyskie wanders around the central, tallest tower, her armour flashing, her flaxen hair static in the breezeless computer air. She can see for miles, over the market, the village, and the two neighbouring castles (one of them Bernard's), and out into the deep green forest, a mass of barely defined colour which, if she scrolls sideways, fills the whole screen with a luminous dark green. She leaves that screen on, dreaming in the background, when she gets up to make herself a cup of tea or an omelette, or to sort through her single-person's laundry. It makes a nice addition to her living room, with its heavy furniture and dusty TV; the pictures of flowers done by a real artist, a volunteer at the hospital; the pile of letters asking her to Save the Children or buy a LOVEFiLM subscription, and the one giving the details of the appointment which she has to go to today. Because now, she has a second secret.

Only Dr Patel knows this secret.

Dr Patel works in the same hospital as Mrs Świętokrzyskie, but in a little white room very different to Mrs Świętokrzyskie's geriatric wards which are enormous, lines of old people stretching so far she can't see to the end of one when she's standing at the door. Dr Patel stumbles over her name, nothing like the clear international sound of her own. Mrs Świętokrzyskie thinks that glossy black hair must look beautiful when it's let down.

Dr Patel bites her lip like a child. 'Mrs Svetoskushky, I'm afraid your tests didn't return very p-positive results. Unfortunately, I have to tell you that there is severe hypertrophic cardiomyopathy at the septum below the aortic valve.'

Mrs Świętokrzyskie looks at her.

'In your heart. A stiffening of the walls of the heart. Now, this is a difficult situation to manage. We'll do . . . I'll do, our very best.'

Mrs Świętokrzyskie's face is still. She's thinking to herself that a Revivor potion could take care of that, or at the most, a hundred dollars forked over to see the Wise Woman.

'A transplant?' she says out loud.

The doctor flushes. Mrs Świętokrzyskie hadn't

known that Indians could go that colour. 'Yes, that would be ideal, Mrs Svetusky, but unfortunately . . . the waiting list is quite long. And, ahem, unfortunately preference is given to younger patients. Also, well, to non-smokers.'

Mrs Świętokrzyskie fondles the thin cigarette packet and cartoon-coloured lighter in her skirt pocket. She's more scared than she'd thought she would be. 'I stopped to smoke in 1991,' she tells Dr Patel. 'But unfortunately I started again. In the year 2000.'

She imagines the golden leopards back home, prowling around the castle, gleaming. Waiting for her.

At WHSmith she buys a will form wrapped in cellophane. After some hesitation she leaves the flat to Gabriela. Josef is the child she loves the most, he's the one she thinks about, but Gabriela sounds so ragged down the phone, and that bony flat in Glasgow hasn't got room to swing a cat.

> I leave in my Last Will and Testament my Flat to my Daughter Gabriela and her Children.
> To Josef my Son I leave my Bank Account and the Contents when I am decease. Also any Contents of the House that he want if Gabriela is agreeable.

That's the right way to put it. She suspects Josef will take the TV and computer, and maybe her mobile phone, but specifying those sounds sad. She doesn't want to quibble over possessions with her children from beyond the grave. She looks at her form, then adds another gift: a secret one written in smaller, scratchier handwriting.

Next to her bed – the big musty marital bed – there's a bedside table. On the bedside table are her glasses, a sprig of lavender and a mug of water for the night. There's a little drawer in the underside of the bedside table, and in it is Mrs Świętokrzyskie's will, and a sealed white envelope with Bernard's full name on it above the words: STRICLY PRIVET AND CONFIDENTAL. Inside that, there's a little piece of paper with Mrs Świętokrzyskie's MagiKingdom username and password written on it carefully, in blue ink.

The next night, she sits again in her big green armchair, battling with someone called Lady Pomona, a blonde with a tall red pointed hat and feathery wings, far below her skill level. Bernard isn't online tonight.

Mrs Świętokrzyskie moves her hand to the mouse to double-click on the weak point in Lady Pomona's armour, the spot where her right wing joins her body – and she's stopped by the sight of her own physical wrist, which seems to be glowing. She sees her own hands every day, but now the joint is getting whiter and whiter as she looks at it, as if her skeleton has come outside her body.

She stares and stares, ignoring the computer's faint hisses of defeat. Up in Yorkshire, Bernard's hand switches on his monitor. His feet twitch in comfy slippers. In ten years he'll be as old as Mrs Świętokrzyskie, the folds of silk lying underneath his skin will rise to the surface.

The white light of Mrs Świętokrzyskie's wrist reaches the white light coming from the flashing screen and unites with it. Her hair fizzes and the veins in her hands crackle. The blood bunches up at a critical, delicate point and something in her brain goes *phut,* as the hand drops to a stop on the fluttering keyboard and lies still. Too slowly to see, her flesh begins losing its pinkness. Underneath, ridging the hand, her bones are still irradiated with life.

It wasn't her heart in the end, not that thickening aortic valve, which let her down. It was a brain aneurysm, the type that no one can predict or prevent. It could have struck her twenty years ago, or passed her by completely and gone on to her new next-door-neighbour, the Ethiopian woman whose kids leave their toy cars out in the hall.

The unexpected aneurysm makes the will in the bedside drawer look very odd, for a few days. Josef mutters darkly about it until his sister finds Dr Patel's name on her mother's kitchen calendar and calls in, and finds out how short Mrs Świętokrzyskie's life expectancy was, anyway.

If you touched the small window in the alley now and peered into Mrs Świętokrzyskie's flat, it would look quite different. The magazines are gone and the pink lamp is inside a cardboard box. The computer monitor sits in Mrs Świętokrzyskie's armchair, its cables tangled around it like a rose thicket around Sleeping Beauty's castle.

A tall dark man and a blonde pregnant woman are moving around. Obviously they don't live here. Their body language shows they're annoyed by the clutter, the flowered wallpaper, even small things like the hard-boiled eggs in the fridge or the meter on the boiler.

Josef picks up a letter. 'This is mine, anyway. She left me the bank account. Didn't she always say she was saving for a rainy day?'

'Josef, don't open her post.' Gabriela doesn't think he'll take any notice of her. She's justified, because opening the letter does him no good.

'Forty-five fucking pounds and fifty pence?'

'No, it can't be – Mum had a load saved up.' Then Gabriela looks more carefully at the bank statement. She heaves a cardboard box of Mrs Świętokrzyskie's possessions up onto her hip as if it's a child. 'Chriiiiiist . . .'

Josef addresses the paper at arm's length. 'What the fuck . . . ? The last thing on here is sixty quid to something called "MagiKingdom". . .' He scowls at Gabriela; a handsome man but failing a little around the chin, whose rough bristle doesn't quite disguise his face's downwards slope. 'Did she buy Maggie a load of toys or something?'

'No, she didn't . . . Look, Joe, here they are again. Oh look, and there. God, two hundred quid that time . . . And there's a subscription fee here too.'

'"Oh look"? That's all you can say? Who's Mum been giving all her money to?'

'Alright. Alright. We can look into this. Let's just Google it. Maybe it's a company, something to do with her illness. You never know.'

They set the computer up again, but when Gabriela presses the round button to power it up, a window flashes up that hasn't been closed since Mrs Świętokrzyskie's death. The avatar that appears doesn't have a human face: instead a peacock's beak tilts towards the screen. Artificial green eyes shine.

WELCOME ZELDA, says the screen. SELECT TO CONTINUE PLAY.

That screen stays up for quite a long time. Gabriela's instinct, and then Josef's, is to log in. But the log-in requires a password, and they have no idea. They didn't know that their sixty-three year old mother lived in a world with passwords. What on earth might she have chosen?

The security question is 'Where did you meet your partner?' Not 'What is your job?' or 'Which of your daughters is dead?' They can't answer it – after trying POLAND, and then, as a possibility, WORK, they give up.

'I'm finding out what this shit is, anyway.'

With blunt fingers Josef types a new username for himself. His sister stands behind him, head tilted to one side, her hand on her hip, as he starts to explore the MagiKingdom.

Gabriela breathes down the phone. 'God, Joe . . . It's serious money.'

On her marble-texture kitchen counter is an open red-topped tabloid announcing a new MagiKingdom record. Apparently a lot of people know about MagiKingdom, though it's never registered in Gabriela's life before. One item, a red jewelled sword called The Terminator, has just sold for $20,000 at an online auction.

Twenty-thousand dollars? Does their dead mother have one of those, tucked behind her sharp-beaked avatar, behind the mysteries she's left as hurdles?

Even if she doesn't, Josef's already established that a MagiKingdom user can put a big chunk into buying armour, potions, fortifications for their castle – and none of them last for long without needing renewing.

'Why did she just flush it all away?' he moans.

'She always felt pretty secure, I guess. Dad's pension was for her life – and she had the flat.'

'What are you trying to say?'

'What? She left me the flat; she left you the bank account.'

'But there's nothing fucking in the bank account!'

'Well . . .'

'Don't say that like that, Ela. There must be a mistake. Either that, or it had already got to her brain.'

'Joe, just 'cause you were her favourite, doesn't mean she was blind. She knew if you had the flat or any decent sum, you'd rip through it in a year –'

Josef hangs up.

He pays a hundred pounds to ask a solicitor if the will is valid, after all.

Mr Moncrieffe says that DIY will forms are carefully designed to be legally binding. 'What they want to do is, they want to make the procedure accessible.' He does note, when Josef is almost out of the door, that the will contains one unexplained legacy that Josef seems to have overlooked. The envelope, a sealed envelope which is mentioned, and the instructions to send it on to an address in Huddersfield . . .?

Josef tells him he's already sent the letter on, when they'd first read the will, he'd thought nothing of it. 'I thought it was personal stuff – you know, sentimental stuff. Maybe she had family there, or old friends . . .'

Mr Moncrieffe smiles and begins to speculate inside his head.

Later Josef leans against Mrs Świętokrzyskie's hall table. He pulls her shining white landline so close into his face that the flesh around his mouth is almost swallowing it. He calls Directory Enquiries, then the Huddersfield phone number they give him. *Bernard Davies.* Such an English name.

'So Klara was your mam. Yes, she left me the account. I s'pose's worth a bit, yes – there's a good trade in MagiParts. And then there's the knapsack . . .'

'Excuse me. What the fuck did you just say?'

The funeral was only five years ago. That was when Josef had dumped his girlfriend, left his flat and moved back in with his mother to the room they'd all shared when they were small, still filled with Ela's university textbooks, Władysława's dolls and the secret condoms she'd left in the bottom drawer of the Ikea dressing table. None of it had been touched since Władysława had stopped calling.

Now after almost a decade of worry and not knowing, of seeing her face pinned up in every phone box, topping the naked models in every tabloid, behind every waving copy of the *Big Issue*, Josef knew where his sister was. She was in the ground. Gabriela left baby Tomasz – no Magda then – in Scotland for the funeral, and she and Josef led their mother away past the grave, past the haze of yellow chrysanthemums. They told her that none of it was her fault, and that they'd look after her forever.

Josef breaks up with the current girlfriend, so he can concentrate. He pays another two hundred pounds to Mr Moncrieffe to find out if leaving someone passwords, leaving them passwords which contain all your wealth and lock it forever away from your children, is really legal.

But Bernard has in his server a whole host of emails, with kisses at the end, indicating that Mrs Świętokrzyskie was of sound mind when she left him what amounts to all her money, that he knew her, that this isn't the kind of fraud that's illegal. Josef imagines Huddersfield as a dark cave, black and damp and burrowed deep into the earth; Bernard as an elderly dragon guarding his mother's treasures, which he has no right to. He telephones Bernard until the Huddersfield police ring the Rotherhithe station, who threaten him with a restraining order.

Bernard Davies sits down heavily in his ergonomic chair. He can feel himself getting older now every time he sits down, and it's worse in this dark basement. But this is where he set up the computer, years ago before Carol left, and moving it has always seemed like too much work.

He feels bad for the boy, the man, who keeps calling. He shouldn't have dropped his sister into the conversation like that. He supposes he'd known that Władysława was the name of Klara's dead child, but they'd both used it so frequently to refer to the castle that he'd stopped really thinking about it. Himself, he'd named his castle 'Ambrosia', a nice fancy-sounding name that reminded him of the tinned custard Carol used to serve with ginger cake. These foreign names just sound grander.

He's told Josef, 'Your mother was a very special lady.' Tried to make him see reason. But the man began yelling and cursing, using bad language, and Bernard replaced the phone neatly on the receiver.

Now he hesitates before launching MagiKingdom, using Klara's account. He goes to Władysława and walks about the battlements just like Klara used to. The wind ruffles his golden hair and the white mink around his collar. Below, in the green forest, the army of leopards turn and snarl. In the distance he sees Ambrosia, the castle belonging to his second self.

He leans forward and looks right into the screen. The avatar which used to be Klara leans forward too, a mirror image. He scrolls to bring it close up. The face is a peculiar creation: a young woman's eyes and forehead – the eyes wide, long-lashed, green, the forehead creamy-white – but underneath, the savage steel beak. The combination is what first drew Bernard to her. Not just a young lass, perhaps one who'd be after calling the police if he spoke to her, or her mam would. A peacock. A peacock in mink furs. A peacock in mink furs and a metal breastplate, with beautiful eyes.

The avatar walks forward into Władysława, passing down the great hall, ignoring the servants who duck out of her way. Somewhere inside the graphics, the screen glare reflects a thin version of Bernard's true face, his shaggy beard and unlovable lips. Somewhere inside Władysława, safe as a womb, is Mrs Świętokrzyskie.

The Works of Lesser-Known Artists

Janet H Swinney

'Fucking toast! Fucking toaster!' The time was up, but the lever stayed down and the toast hadn't appeared. The thing had jammed again. Patti seized the machine, turned it upside down and gave it a vigorous shake. A shower of blackened crumbs sprayed across the draining board and bounced onto her grey work skirt. She dusted them off the thin, ungiving fabric with the back of her hand. The stuff had already acquired bobbles after just a few turns in the dryer. 'Get yourself in here. Now!' she yelled. A door thumped at the end of the passage. Patti had used the 'f' word so often recently that her upper teeth had begun to settle in readiness in a groove on her lower lip. 'I said *now!*' she bellowed. She waggled a knife blade in the slots of the toaster, and finally prised out two crumpled slices of unevenly singed bread.

The kitchen door opened.

'Your tea's made, and there's your toast,' Patti pointed. Shevonne eyed the carboniferous remains momentarily then prized open the biscuit tin and swept half a dozen coconut fingers straight into the mouth of her shoulder bag.

'Tea?' enquired Patti.

Shevonne shrugged. 'Get can,' she said.

'That's not a good use of your pocket money.'

'So?'

Patti felt her upper lip prickle. Shevonne had turned into a belligerent teenager completely unlike the good-natured child Patti had been used to. She resented everything her mother did – or didn't – do. Entirely morose at home, she was a completely different creature once she got outside with her friends. On more than one occasion Patti had spotted a gaggle of them dragging each other about the paved court of the shopping centre, assaulting one another in that contemporary urban patois that was the verbal equivalent of pepper spray. Shevonne, Patti noted, had been at the heart of affairs. The fact was: Patti didn't know how to handle her. Her only strategy was patience, and that was in increasingly short supply. She wondered how many more years she would have to endure before Shevonne evolved into someone half decent.

And then there was the matter of what Shevonne was wearing. Just what was the school's policy on uniform these days? Patti struggled to remember the most recent circular. Surely the stretch-velour tracksuit that left the navel uncovered was well beyond the limits? Shevonne was not built the way her mother had been at the same age.

Patti was a hefty woman now, but in her youth she'd been straight up and down. Shevonne, on the other hand, was already well developed. Her bosom was large, and her buttocks gyrated like two boulders in a bag when she walked. She had heavy thighs that made her belly look as though it was in retreat, and a compact pubic area that formed a narrow, downward arrow in between. Her body could be read as one simple message, and that was: an invitation to try your hand. This was a message the tracksuit did nothing to repudiate.

Patti started to form words that would broach the subject, but then the radio spoke: *Five to eight.* No time to deal with this now. She would have to try and remember to bring it up later. She rammed a plastic box containing an already-weary sandwich into her shopping bag and then stuffed in a couple of carriers. She would need to get to the market in her lunch break. *And* the post office. She ran through the list of things she needed: vegetables of course, pan scourers, a bra for herself – oh! – and she must get some cooking apples. She was planning on doing something with them tonight for dessert. 'Right,' she said. 'Out!' She shooed Shevonne out on to the landing then, following closely on her heels, and slammed the door of their flat behind them.

A crush of anxious people fidgeted at the bus stop. The numbers on the overhead indicator board tickered by, seemingly at random. Six minutes, four, eighteen, two. Crouch End, Friern Barnet, Holloway. None of them was what she needed. She'd already been late three times this month thanks to breakdowns, stoppages and diversions. She couldn't afford to be late again: her appraisal was looming. To take her mind off the consequences of a 'does not meet expectations' rating, she stared at the overflowing rubbish bin next to the bus stop. It had been an unusually long summer with a gritty heat that got into your pores and a blustering breeze that brought no relief. The discarded chicken carcasses, crushed cans and greasy cartons, a testimony to the previous evening in the inner city, were already stinking. Splotches of chewing gum spattered the paving, and a potpourri of prematurely crushed autumn leaves and cigarette butts whirled intermittently in the gutter. Patti blinked. She could already feel perspiration creeping between her cheap and cheerful canerows.

She wasn't late, but only by good luck. She took up her place in an upper salon next to Exhibit One. Ivan sloped past her, well off the beaten track for Mediaeval Armour.

'Wa'ppun?' she said.

'Researching a novel. Arthurian legend meets Australian outback. It's all up here.' Ivan tapped the side of his head where the long, knotted scar scythed through his greasy locks.

'Look forward to hearing more about it,' Patti said. Ivan disappeared.

There were only a handful of early morning

pensioners doing the rounds, making the most of their exhibition passes. Patti would have liked to have sat down after her gruelling journey – she'd had to stand all the way on the lower deck, and already her ankles were beginning to inflate – but that had been forbidden. Since that chap had made off in broad daylight with a Persian amphora and an Anglo-Saxon comb there'd been a change of regime. The fact that he'd been caught trying to sell the stuff on eBay had made matters worse. It had made the top managers look utter damn fools. So now you were supposed to stand all day looking as though you were 'on your toes'. Patti eyed the stool that still stood by the entrance to the room. Perhaps she could just slide one buttock on?

There had been other changes too. They'd all been issued with 'walkie-talkies' and were supposed to use them to transmit surveillance messages to each other. The old, reactionary trade unionists and the young, avant-garde postgraduates talking to each other in alphabet spaghetti: 'Alpha, Foxtrot, Charlie. Come in, come in. Bacon sandwiches now available at the Monmouth Street entrance.' Within about a fortnight, eighteen handsets had either been stolen in mysterious circumstances or accidentally dropped down stairwells.

Then there was the uniform. The new Head of Customer Service had come from some northern constabulary, nothing to do with Art at all, and decreed that their kit needed an overhaul. Now they were all dressed like members of the Metropolitan

Police force. The women wore blazers with jaunty cravats that clipped on under the collars of their polyester shirts. The ill-fitting blazers were bad enough, but worst of all were the shirts which were far too thin, freezing in winter and broiling in summer, and which revealed every detail of your underwear. The young women turned this to their advantage, wearing elaborately corniced balcony bras to instigate flirtation with the visitors. But for larger-chested, older women like Patti, it was a nightmare. She didn't like being on display: people were supposed to be looking at the Art, not at her. And she somehow felt that unruly breasts might let her down – that their conduct was being appraised as well as hers. What she needed was some serious breast management.

The trickle of visitors gained a steady momentum. She was patrolling a temporary exhibition: *The Works of Lesser-Known Artists: Surrealism Revisited*. She stood in front of the introductory panel, reading again some of the smart-smart stuff that was written there. The six featured artists were: Gérard de Forcalquier, Pascal Thierry, Guy Sans-Sens, Florent de Haute Ville, Jean-Paul Gascon and Emile de Vouvray. All had been featured in or contributed to a little-known journal called *La Fenêtre Ouverte*. There was much about life on the edge and the years the artists had spent in fevered introspection in clubs and cafés. One of them had committed suicide and another had attempted it. Alongside was a portrait of them, a group of po-faced men in horse-hair suits and starched collars doing things they thought were witty with bananas. The text ended with a quote from an actor: 'Surrealism is not a style. It is the cry of a mind turning back on itself . . .' Patti sucked her teeth. She had her doubts.

Two pensioners approached. 'We're puzzled by this painting,' they said. Patti followed them over to the painting in question, a series of dotted lines, attenuated eyebrows and unfinished business entitled, *Un Portrait de Madame F. et Son Chien*. 'Where's the dog?' asked the elderly woman. 'Only, we've got a terrier, and we can't see it,' said the man. There was no bloody dog. Patti pointed at a ball of scribble floating in the bottom right-hand corner. 'Some critics think this is the dog,' she said. 'If you look carefully you can just make out marks that allude to what might be eyes and a tail.' The pensioners were satisfied. They thanked her and moved on.

When she'd landed this job, she'd been filled with enthusiasm. It was such a change from working in the dry cleaner's, keeping track of tickets and inhaling petroleum fumes all day long. Not to mention the string of other worthless jobs she'd had, cleaning offices, serving behind bars and working on the switchboard at Duke's Taxi Cabs. She'd really thought she'd be able to make good use of the diploma, Art and Counter-Culture, that she'd embarked on years ago at Goldsmiths, and which she'd had to abandon when she'd fallen pregnant with Shevonne. She'd even considered resuming her studies, perhaps doing a couple of evening classes in Art History to improve her job satisfaction and increase her promotion prospects. In reality, she'd had to work such long hours to make a living wage, aspiration had begun to wither on the vine. Regime change had finished it off.

A teacher arrived with a party of Spanish school children. What the heck were they going to make of some of this stuff? The teacher caught her eye. 'Don't worry,' she said, 'I've got workbooks for them.'

Patti followed them round at a slow pace, revisiting works she'd looked at many times before: in the middle of the room, a series of spinning discs and spindles that played the music of Varèse when you pressed a button, plus a rotating dentist's chair complete with patient, a concoction of papier-mâché, wire and some unsavoury scraps of synthetic fur. Every time the chair passed a trigger point, the patient's mouth opened to 180 degrees and he emitted a terrible scream – the kids might like that at least. Then the paintings on the walls: one showing segments of a female torso hanging on a tree shaped like a Glam Rock hairdo; a woman with ferocious eyebrows, a tuning fork for a nose and a slapped-on kipper for a mouth; a grey, whale-shaped blob on stilts that Thierry had entitled *Sous La Mamelle de Ma Mère*; a creature of Gascon's imagining that was half-woman, half-downturned scissors, the finger grips representing her ovaries, the blades the extraordinarily long lips of her vulva. What was wrong with these men? What explained the fact that they seemed to know so little about women and appreciate them even less?

She felt a particular hatred for *La Rêve d'une Négresse Verte* by de Haute Ville. With its vibrant colours, the work dominated one end of the room. It depicted the head and shoulders of woman with features similar to her own, set against a tropical landscape. The woman's eyes were closed. But she had substance only as far up as her lower lip. After that, her head became a spiral of vegetable peel, opening up ever wider, to reveal a broadening expanse of the flora behind her, until it trailed off into the sky. In other words: it was empty. Patti stood glaring at the piece for a good ten minutes. Then she became aware that the cluster of people behind her was growing, so she moved on to let them get a better view.

The whole thing depressed her. She was standing fuming by the fire extinguisher, inventing a few titles for alternative art works of her own – *Husband Pisses next to Cenotaph*, *Bitch Takes a Step Too Far*, *Six Meat Dumplings Orbit Ceiling Fan*, and *Suitcase Contemplates a Rubbish Chute* – when she felt her mobile phone tremble in her pocket. It was a text: 'Shevonne is not in school today. This is an unauthorised absence.' What? This was a new development. Not Shevonne absenting herself: that had happened often enough before. But the fact that the school could, would dare to, invade her privacy by text. When had she even given them her mobile phone number? She struggled to read the rest of the message. 'Secretary of State for Education . . . legal requirement . . . parental responsibility . . . subject to fine . . .' Dear God, how would she pay any fine? She could barely afford to buy margarine to scrape onto their bread and off it again. She swore at the Secretary of State for Education. Just what was she supposed to do to get her truculent adolescent through the school gate every day? It was hard enough getting her out of the house. Her heart sank at the prospect of the evening of ugliness that lay ahead. She would get home knackered, and then she would have to confront Shevonne not just about the tracksuit, but about the matter of skiving off again. This time all the more serious because of the prospect of a fine.

She spent her break in the staff restroom, when she would much rather have listened to Ivan rambling on about his novel, trying to contact her daughter. Needless to say, there was no response. She slipped a chocolate Penguin into her mouth, and followed it with another. With a couple of minutes to go, Eileen from Oriental Textiles plonked herself down next to her.

'Thought you were trying to cut down?'

'Now never seems to be the right time,' said Patti. 'Soon I won't be able to get this skirt on.'

'Friggin' uniform,' commented Eileen, who had opted for the trousered version of the outfit. I've got gay women all over me like flies on shit.'

Back on the floor, Patti cruised past Forcalquier's sculpture, *Motion Perpétuelle*, an assemblage of female body parts with no head that, cleverly, could be fucked from every angle. 'Fragmentation, dismemberment; dismemberment, reassembly: the cycle is interminable and inevitable', the caption read. She was watching Japanese students assiduously copying this down when her handset crackled.

'Beat Seventeen, come in, come in.'

'Yes. Hello, I'm here.'

'Beat Seventeen?'

'Yes, yes.'

'You should use the proper form of address.'

'Can't remember it,' said Patti sullenly.

The person on the other end clicked her tongue. 'Delta Five and Delta Six would like to see you now. Beat Twenty-One will relieve you.' Lorraine and Ursula, the Queens of Mean of staff supervision. Another couple of bright young appointees who were a feature of regime change, and who took their new-found responsibilities far too seriously. One of their greatest acts of altruism was nailing Stanley, the shop steward, on a disciplinary charge, within six months of his retirement. Now he was sitting at home, suspended, sweating about whether or not he was going to get his pension.

What could this be about? Ah, perhaps it was the request for Christmas leave she'd put in weeks ago. It would be a big family do in Kingston, and probably the last chance she'd have to see her dying father. She'd already taken out a loan and bought the air tickets before the prices got way beyond her.

She rushed down darkened corridors in the basement to find the pair of them.

'Hello, Patti,' said Lorraine silkily from behind the desk they shared. Patti smiled brightly, if somewhat unconvincingly. 'What it is: we need you to work Sunday.'

That knocked the smile off Patti's face. 'I've already worked five in a row.'

'Can't be helped,' cooed Lorraine, brushing something invisible off the lapel of her narrow jacket, and flicking her sleek brown hair over her shoulder. 'There'll be a big party in for a special event.'

Patti decided to take a stand. 'No, really. I have things to see to at home, and I need to spend some time with my daughter. Ask someone else.'

'We know you need the money,' said Lorraine, stiffening. 'You should be grateful for the opportunity. We don't offer it to everyone. And what's more,' she said, 'Ursula saw you sitting down this morning.' Ursula pursed her perfectly pink lips and nodded.

'I only . . .' began Patti, remembering the one buttock.

'Backside in contact with surface of chair,' said Ursula brusquely. 'It's called sitting down. If you don't work this Sunday, we'll put it on your record.' With her long pastel fingernails she picked at a corner of the buff-coloured folder in front of her.

'Jeez-us!' the word squeezed out from between Patti's teeth. 'And what about my Christmas leave?'

'We haven't made our minds up yet,' said Ursula.

'Time's getting on,' whispered Patti.

'Mmmm,' said Lorraine, languidly. 'Still thinking it over.'

'Cha! What bitches!' fumed Patti as she rushed through the back streets at lunch time. 'Let them kiss mi backside!' Still, she couldn't afford to dwell on the morning's incident. She needed to get to the market as fast as possible. There was a chap at the far end who specialised in underwear for the larger woman. She made straight for him.

'I want something with plenty of reinforcement,' she said.

'As in "Send reinforcements, we're going to a dance?"'

'Eh? No.' On another occasion, she might have had a joke with him, but today she was too hard-pressed to appreciate the levity.

'Never mind, love. It was probably before your time,' said the trader. He rummaged among the hangers on his rail and brought out an item to show her. He removed the cellophane wrapper. The bra was a bastion of buttresses, broad straps and ample cup coverage yet somehow, with a carapace of crusty nylon net, it still managed a feminine appearance. Patti sized it up.

'Got it in red as well, if you fancy a bit of

passion,' said the trader. He raised a flirtatious eyebrow.

Patti looked at him frostily. 'Black will do me nicely. How much?'

'Tenner.'

'Eight.'

'Two for eighteen.'

She couldn't afford two. She would have to take one and wash it out every night. She got the original for nine.

She fought her way back between the backsides and baby buggies of people who had more time on their hands to do their shopping than she did, queued at the fruit and vegetable stall and took on a load of apples, carrots and bananas, and then set a course for the last leg – destination post office – to pick up her Child Benefit. Just as she passed the homeware stall with its pyramids of pans; teetering towers of Pyrex, and boxes of knock-off washing-up liquid, the trader got up on his perch and started his pitch:

'The most useful thing in your kitchen. Quality steel, straight from Germany. Opens bottles, opens cans. Will core an apple. Will peel a potato. Will even take the eyes out for you, if you ask it nicely. Quick as a flash. See!' He held up a complicated looking object. It had a corer at one end, and a traditional bottle opener at the other. But, cleverly, the bottle opener had an additional prong for puncturing cans. The trader flourished the item for effect and then eviscerated a cooking apple. 'Come on, now, only a dozen of these left to go.'

Patti stopped in her tracks. The very thing!

'One for four-fifty, two for seven. Buy one for yourself, buy one for your mate, buy one for your daughter.'

The magic words! A novelty gadget like that would certainly appeal to Shevonne. It might even persuade her to give a hand with making the dinner, and then they could get talking, and then . . .

Patti pushed her way to the front of the gathering. She fumbled in her purse and flashed the guy a fiver. A gadget was quickly handed over. It was too much of a challenge to get it into her bag, so she dropped it into the pocket of her blazer. Perfect! Now, heaving to, she steered her way towards the post office.

The atmosphere in the post office was oppressive. The place was full, but the Indian couple behind the counter ran it with all the languid hauteur of colonial bureaucracy, taking a dead-weight of time to do anything. The long queue inched painfully towards the counter amid sighs and coughs, and women menacing their fractious children.

Patti nudged her bags along the floor with the side of her shoe. Her feet felt like jars of potted salmon now, and she moved her weight from one foot to another to try and relieve the burning sensation. She had her eyes on the clock above the counter. The pointers were jerking round steadily towards the witching hour when her lunch break would be over and she would, once again, be at risk of reprisals. 'Come on, come on!' she muttered. A smoker with a lot of tar on his chest embarked on a long cough that sounded like the rattle of maracas. A toddler got entangled in the tape that was supposed to keep the customers in order, and set up a loud, penetrating wail. Patti considered leaving the matter for another day. But she couldn't: she couldn't last without the money. She would have to take her chances.

The pointer on the clock jerked another notch and wobbled. The door swung open. A man in a wheelchair glided in and, deftly manoeuvring the controls on the armrest, circumvented the queue and made for the counter. The man had no legs, just flaps of trouser folded up and safety-pinned. He looked untroubled either by his condition or the winding ribbon of people.

'For Chrissake!' thought Patti, clenching her hands. 'If that bastard thinks he's getting served before me, he can think again. I'll rip his arms off.' Then she caught herself mid-sentiment, and was horrified. She had just completed her NVQ module in Equality and Diversity. Where had all that gone then? What was life doing to her? She was losing sight of herself. She spent every waking moment trying, fighting to hold everything together. She had no time for anything: no time for herself, no time for her daughter and now, no time even for compassion. Her whole existence was absurd. And what did it amount to? Nothing.

The man in the wheelchair took a couple of

information leaflets and a form and veered out again. There was a collective sigh.

At last, with the press of people behind her, it was Patti's turn to wash up at the counter. She rested there like a beached whale while she felt inside her shoulder bag. The man behind the grille looked over his spectacles at her and parted his lips in what wasn't exactly a smile. 'Child Benefit,' Patti said. She pushed her hand deeper into her bag. The small wallet that held her payment card wasn't in its usual place. There was a pocket she kept especially for that, but it wasn't there. The man raised an eyebrow and moved his pen from one side of his blotting pad to the other. Now Patti felt around frantically. She could hear muttering and the impatient shuffling of feet behind her. Sweat broke out on the back of her neck. She panicked. She started to turn her bag out.

'It's here. I know it's here.'

'Aw, come on,' someone said, as a set of keys fell out and a lipstick rolled across the floor, 'shift your arse.'

She fled.

She stood at the crossing on the busy main road waiting for the lights to change, with her ton-weight carrier bags wrenching her arms from their sockets. She had no explanation for what had just happened. That wallet was never anywhere else but in her bag. So had it moved into the fifth dimension, or was she losing her marbles? An immense truck thundered past creating a downdraft that nearly knocked her over, sand-blasting her face with grit and pulling tears from the corners of her eyes. Now she was out of money and almost out of time.

She got into the back door of the gallery with seconds to spare. She swiped herself in, rammed her shopping into her locker and slung her walkie-talkie back on her shoulder. Her sandwich remained wilting in its box. She should really be back upstairs by now, but she was desperate for a wee.

The wee cost her valuable minutes and back on the beat among *The Works of Lesser-Known Artists*, Ivan, who'd been holding the fort, was champing at the bit.

'Sorry, mate. I've had an awful lunch time.'

'You and me both,' he said. 'It's hell in here.'

The place was packed. An ill-tempered throng of seasoned exhibition-goers stuck their elbows in each other's sides and flung their jackets in each other's faces, as they jostled for viewing positions. The benches were full of people resting their feet and refusing to budge. College students were crouched on the floor in positions of submission, sketching in their notebooks, hoping that accuracy of observation would enhance their grade profile at some point down the line. The temperature had soared, and the place smelled of many varieties of sweat. Why hadn't management decided on regulated entry for such a prestigious exhibition? But then that was the policy these days: 'Stack 'em up, sell 'em high'.

Patti did a slow round of the room, thwarting a couple of children intent on sticking their fingers into the fuckable sculpture, and giving directions to a young couple with unintelligible English who seemed to be in the wrong gallery altogether. The dental patient was howling his head off and the Varèse was jangling away relentlessly.

Patti approached *La Rêve d'une Négresse Verte*. The riven eyes of the woman in the picture seemed to be closed in prayer, asking mutely for release from her torture. For a moment, as she stood there in her boil-in-the-bag blazer and cling-film shirt, with her feet puffed up over the edges of her shoes and perspiration trickling down over the rolls of fat on her back, Patti joined her in a plea for liberation. Then her handset made a noise like the sound of chips entering the fryer.

'Beat Seventeen, come in, come in.'

'Yes. What?'

'I said, "Beat Seventeen . . ."'

'I know what you said. And I said, "What?"'

'It's Delta Five here.'

'I know it's Delta Five. What do you want?'

'You should say, "How can I help you?"'

'How can I help you, Lorraine?' How old was she again?

'You were late this afternoon.'

'I wasn't late. Check the time clock.'

'Delta Six saw you. You were late on to the beat.'

'I had to go to the toilet, that's all.' She was forty-five and she was trying to justify having a wee.

'Well, anyway, we've made our minds up.'

Patti stayed silent.

'I said we've made our minds up.'

'Oh?' Patti knew what was coming.

'We've decided No. We can't give you the time off at Christmas.'

'You can't give me time off to see a man who's dying?'

'No. The rosters are very tight. Later in the year would suit us better.'

'Did you not hear what I said?' Patti started. 'I . . .' then she snapped the phone off. What was the point? Suddenly, both hope and hopelessness dropped away from her like barrels rolling overboard into a tranquil sea. She had nothing to lose and there was nothing she could gain. Instead, a force that she had never known before stepped into her shoes, and swept through her like a tidal wave. Time expanded. Like an off-spin bowler coming in from the Vauxhall end, she took her arm right back in her awkward jacket, and flung the handset with full force onto the floor. It shattered, sending bits of plastic skittering between people's shoes. But in the midst of bedlam, only a few people close at hand noticed this aberration . . . and moved on.

Now she placed herself squarely in front of the painting. She watched herself stand strong, indomitable and tall. She had never felt so powerful. She was raised up! Whether through the mysteries of Obeah or of God Almighty Himself, she did not know. But, oh Lord, she was raised up! Somewhere in the background, a small, fearful, submissive self was wittering away neurotically. Her strong self dismissed it. Coolly, she fingered the gadget in her blazer pocket, testing the prong against her thumb. This thing had been purpose-built for the job in hand, and she knew exactly what to do.

She stepped over the rope that kept the pictures from the public. She sank the fang firmly into the canvas, and drew a strong diagonal right to left across the picture. She followed it with another and then another. Then others, left to right. The woman with the peeled cranium fell with relief from her frame in fragments that rolled slowly to the floor. The ripping sensation that reached through the blade and up into Patti's arm was wonderful; the scorching, tearing sound was glorious. Truly, she had stepped beyond herself into a world of pure sensation. 'Lord, let me stay in this place of exaltation forever. Let me stay forever.'

But now she felt strong hands hauling her arms roughly behind her back, and heard the thrill of alarms all around. At the edges of her vision, there were faces frowning in disapproval.

She sat in the Director's office. The apple corer-bottle opener thing had, rather unwisely, been left unattended on the desk. She had stopped crying now, but the front of her shirt was wet. Her cravat was missing. She closed her eyes. All she felt was that she felt nothing. 'Surrealism is not a style. It is the cry of a mind turning back on itself.' In her mind's eye, she saw a darkened salon hung with pictures: a cluster of palm trees dripping shadow; a white torrent slicing through a dense green forest; a bowl of orchids in an airy room. She turned from one exhibit to another, studying the detail. Just because the gallery was in her head, did that mean it wasn't real? She waited for some man to come and tell her.

Still Life

Jennifer Obidike

I

When you are lonely and alone, in a city you cannot call home, you might suddenly feel as if anything and everything were possible. You might decide to take off all your clothes.

II

Students trickle in. They assemble themselves quietly, greeting one another for the first time since last term. Easels are set around the room. The tutor weaves herself in and out, arranging tables for coffee and tea, for tins of pastels and shrivelled tubes of paint.

We start with short dynamic poses. The students see me as shapes and negative space, and I am all triangles, unable to move for lengths of time. I burrow into myself, exploring the terrain of my body: a stiffness of arms and throbbing of legs. I focus on my breath, but sometimes I cannot ease into this rhythmic lullaby. Sometimes my thoughts and the people who populate them interfere.

The hazards of life modelling vary from minor

to threatening. They include blackened feet from the brushed-off ashes of charcoal, older men who flit like flies and flatulence in a room full of strangers. One afternoon, on a heavy day of menstruating, a trickle of blood slides down my leg.

The room falls silent as students produce in reverie or consternation. Gemma draws me forth in black ink, an apparition of limbs and bones, her eyes all over my body. They cannot see my small movements but sooner or later they will. Internally, my organs are quivering: my colon contracting and my bladder ready to burst. My mind yelling 'stop' but my body saying 'go'. *What if I have to pee?*

Relaxing into position, I stare blankly out the window. A boy appears, leaning out of his own and peering down below. He disappears and reappears with a broomstick which he throws out the window with glee. He leans dangerously over the sill, looks down and smiles.

At break time students congratulate me, except for Richard who tells me the trembling of my arm annoyed him. I admit to nearly fainting from fear to which he says, 'You've been the most compelling model I've had in a long time.' He reveals the start of his painting: a warrior whose inner child longs to be seen. When he looks at me, I know how it will end, yet I ask him to coffee, anyway.

A focus on the breath causes less anxiety during moments of pain. If I succeed, when the timer dings or the tutor says 'change', then stretching feels sweet. When modelling, I have a stain on the floor or a scratch on the wall — places to rest my eyes as a means of transcendence and in this state, my nudity no longer concerns me. When time is up, students lay down their tools, shedding all concentration. Finally, they see me for what I am.

III

Edward focuses on my face, positioning his easel in front of me and obscuring my point of reference, a yellow sticker placed upon the wall. He opens his wooden case of paints and removes his brushes, bottles and rags. He adjusts and readjusts his canvas. Edward moves this way and that, and after all of his shuffling, the sticker is revealed. My vision blurs. My mind strives towards emptiness, but it is difficult to clear the mind. I wonder what I want for dinner, if I should go to the grocery store for chocolate and bananas.

In and out of the spaces between easels, the tutor weaves, stopping at one student and then another. 'There are warm colours and cool colours. Look at the forehead. Look at the chin. The chin's darker than the forehead. So is the neck, but the chest and breasts are lighter, until you get to the nipples. Look,' she says, taking the student's paintbrush from his hands. 'Look at the patches of darker skin surrounded by the light. Look at her elbows, nipples, crotch. Focus on the contrast now.'

Trivial thoughts layer over nuanced desires.

Scribbled lines and forgotten pieces of masking

tape assault the wall I stare at and in the midst of this chaos lies the sticker: hazardous and neon, flashing 'warning' and 'beware'. The breath settles and my mind drifts into nothingness, pleasurable but fleeting. Last night a breeze rose from the river caressing our faces. Richard and I like teenagers celebrating springtime in London. We sat in silence on a bench in the park, a security car creeping closer (our lips) and closer (our tongues). We paid no mind to the hot white eyes, to the dark, closing hour. We felt verdant, a word connoting nothing but the intoxication of green: cold, wet and youthful green.

Despite our sanctuary, even freedom has limits: amused by sounds of our desire, teenagers have snickered, gates have been locked at closing time and cold winds have reduced us to cowards. In a hotel room, we can moan as loud as we want. Yet my release feels incomplete as I hold back at his impending departure. I withhold my lips; tell him kissing's too intimate. I turn away. I straddle him just as quickly; I lean his head back; I kiss him. My only power appears to be the minutes crouched between his legs where, as he erupts, his breath extinguishes. His fingers clutch my shoulder blades. He believes pleasure absolves him of guilt. A beautiful, young woman frees him of the grief in his heart: a wife who looks at him with daggers and whose speech is laced with venom. He cannot see how he stagnates with each orgasm, each sticky drop of denial. He hands me cash before he leaves because he knows I need it and not because he 'thinks of me in *that way*'. It is when I accept after protestation that I am bruised.

Nudity in an art class is not the same as nudity in front of someone who devours you. An art class expects nothing but stillness. You can be fat or thin, ugly or beautiful, and in all states you are glorified and useful. Thoughts, or a lack of them, clothe you in armour. The first time I took off my clothes for him alone I felt so shy I wanted to put them back on.

IV

There's nothing I love more than the scratchings of charcoal against newsprint. The charcoal snaps from the intensity of the hand that grips it, the other half tinkling when falling to the ground. It is then crushed underfoot by the weight of a body in rapture or disappointment with his or her drawing. The sound of fingers rubbing against paper like acts of vandalism. In overhead light, particles float and sparkle in the air. I have learned that the energy an artist puts into a drawing never matches the desired result, that the artistry I sense while posing is not what's documented when I move to the other side. This, of course, depends on the calibre of the artist, but it is more than I could ever do. There's never enough time to capture a face or an entire body, but there are times when the essence of my pose is lifted from life straight onto the page, either as likeness or radical reimagining.

Victoria beckons for the tutor, perturbed by my legs. My eyes roam, veering away from Edward and the yellow sticker. *I feel I need to pee.*

Can I see you today? I had asked him. *Today isn't a good day,* he'd said. *But when is a good day? I don't know. I'll let you know.*

The window behind Edward frames a scene of trunkless trees. The row houses show their backs, all bricks and windows. My eyes roam, noticing the stiff bodies of easels and the more malleable ones of human beings. In this room full of strangers who I have come to recognise, I tell myself not to cry. If I am not careful, they will see two or three tears falling down the contour of my cheeks – tears I cannot wipe away in my duty to stay still.

V

During break, we chew stale biscuits and drink filtered coffee. I circle the room, curious to see how the students have captured me. Each canvas portrays either a stranger or a version of myself I have met before. In Edward's eyes, I am stern-faced and androgynous. In Gemma's, I am elegant, my back upright, my hands clasped and tucked into my lap. Cynthia captures the child that sometimes radiates from my face. In the twenty minutes we have to socialise, I speak to Margaret who slowly unravels like the bristles of a brush in water. Her red, round earrings bob gently against the lobes of her ears. Edward trips over a chair, knocking over a bottle of Zest. He mumbles under his breath and leans, painfully, to wipe the spill, which begins to perfume the air. Katherine radiates spunk. Cynthia charms me with awkwardness. Victoria, often grave, continues to sketch painstakingly in the corner. Gemma pipes up as soon as I return to pose: the only one who needs the spotlight, chair, hands and feet *exactly* as they were the last time.

The boy returns to the window, launching a pink bucket and then a spade. He turns around, disappears into darkness, comes back and throws down a heavy Persian rug, which takes all of his weight to release. He leans out of the window and I worry he will topple to his death. My bladder pushes; my colon contracts: *what if I have to pee?* My toes rebel with the stop of blood flow, wriggling underneath my thigh. *I have to pee I do not have to pee I have to pee.*

A pool seems to spread beneath me, and as soon as I jerk my head, they will know, and if I pretend, the stench will reach them. Who knows how long I have to go? If I flee they will see the cushion's dark evidence; I move my head, yet nothing is there. Gemma complains that I have moved; Edwards curses under his breath; Cynthia throws me a look of understanding, happy to have a break.

My fear of the boy's death is assuaged by his father who pops his head out the window to see a pile of household goods on the pavement below.

He turns to the boy in the shadows and slams the window shut.

In moments of goodbye, sadness invades my countenance, but sometimes it is a joy to be sad. We have spent hours together yet they know little about me. I have stood naked before them as they wrestled with my 'impossibly endless limbs'. I am who I am. I cannot be defined. They have tried. They have studied me and I have studied them. We may not see each other again. I will miss their smiles of gratitude and the joy on each face. They roll me up and tuck me away, reminding me we all have to die, that there is a time in life when we all have to strive to push away idleness, as we advance in years. Some of us will have the privilege to do what we want, when we have retired, such as draw or paint. Our partners, if we have them, will fall ill and this will consume us, except during moments of creation. I have watched how the ones who are tired or grieving isolate themselves from the group. They do not speak. The others, as if not wanting to catch his or her despair, do not speak to them.

'Time is up,' the tutor says, yet my body's reluctant to move.

VI

The evening of the group show Richard brings his wife and three children. I note the family's formation: how he stands at the forefront resting his hands on the heads of the children as if to claim them, his wife behind, the negative space between them all resembling the bars of a cage. The children stand between the two with what I interpret as longing but who knows what I really see? Richard jokes and makes us laugh, while the blood drains from his wife's face.

The night before I dreamt we went on holiday to Spain. Richard accompanied by his family and I inevitably alone. We had agreed to meet at a café at breakfast time because mornings were a time of innocence, and one denied to lovers. I watched as a cook scooped and flipped omelettes as large and soft as pillows, billows of steam rising from the pockets like long, desirous sighs. Puffing . . . heaving . . . collapsing upon themselves . . . I wanted my fork and knife. I wanted to split into the softness and feel just as guilty as he. He came and stood beside me but did not speak. Just beyond him, on the other side of glass, his wife and children sat; the smallest crawling underneath and the eldest two huddling close. The waitress handed him two plates of fried eggs. He winked at me and walked away. Why had he been served before me? The line was long. Everyone with eggs except for me. I raged as the omelettes were plated, reducing in number, until finally the waitress said, 'I'm sorry, I didn't see you.' By this time he and his family had left. They were cycling away into the Spanish light, spilling onto the streets so brightly it bleached all the colour away. They were figures in a glossy, black-and-white photograph, the five of them on wheels with him at the lead, cycling on a white-drenched street, the picture taken from behind to capture the width of happiness and without needing to see their faces, I knew they were smiling.

Meditation feels like an outline where all the space inside looks precious. There's no need to fill it in. People always want to fill things in. Build things up. Make it heavy. He throws light and shadow onto my existence. He colours me in with cross-hatched strokes. How much easier agony is than stillness, patience and virtue. Sometimes you enter into disastrous situations because you know, later on, you will no longer be the woman on the page here today but another who knows something more.

On Margate Sands

Uschi Gatward

Angela and Lisa sit on the Harbour Arm, eating chips.

The sky looks like the fighting Temeraire. 'Except the sunset is in the wrong place,' says Angela. Lisa, who is used to south coast seaside, suddenly clicks that they are facing north. She gets out her camera, winds it on and takes a photo of her friend, orange hair against the orange sun. And then one holding up a wooden spoon of mushy peas. 'Guacamole,' says Angela to the camera.

They have been here a day. Dreamland has begun its decline, and the Turner gallery will not be built for twenty years. Margate, they agree, is a bit of a waste land.

It's Michaelmas term (although Angela and Lisa do not call it that), and it's not warm. The chips are delicious, wrapped in cornets of paper and soaked in vinegar. Lisa has ketchup on hers, which is 'just wrong,' in Angela's opinion. They eat them all, especially the crunchy bits at the end, unwrapping the cornet to find them.

Lisa takes out a pack of Marlboro Lights, and they promise each other that they will give up once they have finished their dissertations. They huddle together over the flame and then pull their hoods up and scrunch their sleeves into their fists to smoke and watch the day come to an end.

As night falls they walk further into it, east along the esplanade, past the Winter Gardens and the old 1930s Lido, towards Cliftonville, where their B&B is. They dropped off their bags this morning.

At an off-licence along the way they stop and buy cold beer. They smuggle it into the B&B, all net curtains, chintz and china, and a curly 'Vacancies' sign.

They sit on the twin beds drinking lager from cans and looking at the newspaper and the tourist leaflets. The weather forecast is sunny tomorrow, and the clocks go back, which means they will have an extra hour. Angela wants to visit the shell house she remembers from day trips here as a child. Not the Shell Grotto — she looks at the picture and doesn't think they're the same thing. But they can't see any other reference to the shell house, so Lisa says they must be. Lisa wants to go on the Big Wheel.

They force themselves to do an hour's silent reading before bed, *Speech and Phenomena* for Angela, and *Gawain and the Green Knight* for Lisa, making it to forty-five minutes before Angela can't stand it any longer.

Angela talks vaguely about the Derrida essay she is writing. She thinks it will help to talk it through but it doesn't make sense when she tries. She wonders whether she could structure it using the lyrics of the Scritti Politti song, 'Jacques Derrida'. Lisa is doubtful. 'It's a good idea though, isn't it?' says Angela. Lisa grunts.

They smoke their way through Lisa's cigarettes, saving one each for the morning. They get an early night, which means eleven o'clock ('but really ten'), and are up at eight, coughing over the ashtray.

In the empty breakfast room, with its crowded tables and chairs, its artificial stems in vases, they fill themselves up with eggs and bacon, toast and jam.

Angela is excited about her Derrida essay. 'I slept the best sleep I've slept for months,' she says. 'The Scritti Politti was a real breakthrough.'

'Pace yourself,' says Lisa. 'It's not even week four.'

'This is the best meal I've had in weeks,' says Angela. 'I really want a cigarette now though.'

'I saved a bit of mine,' says Lisa, ever-provident, and they share half a chipped Marlboro Light over a refill of coffee.

'Perhaps we could go to a record shop in the afternoon,' says Angela.

This morning, at half past nine, fresh cigarettes lit, they climb down a metal staircase to the beach. They take off their trainers and socks and walk, single file, along the water's edge towards the Main Sands. Sunlight glances off the chalk of the cliffs. They've packed day bags with towels and extra clothes and the tourist guides.

At a small cove just before they reach the Sands they sit down, spreading their towels a few yards from the sea. Apart from a couple of dog walkers, there's no one about. They can hear the quiet lapping of the waves.

'Clacton Pier,' says Angela, pointing. The day is unusually bright, the sun an hour higher in the sky than yesterday.

Lisa cracks open *Gawain* and lies on her stomach to read.

Towards midday they get up and head for the main beach, which is busier with day-trippers.

'Let's go on the Big Wheel now, before we have lunch,' says Lisa.

They cross the road to Dreamland and stand in the queue. As the Wheel empties, it's filled again with the waiting people, winched up pair by pair to let the next carriage drop to the ground. Each carriage is a pendent lantern. Angela and Lisa step into theirs and are shut in with a clank of cold metal. The floor moves under their feet as the lantern stirs on its wire. It all feels madly unsafe.

'We should have got an ice cream,' says Angela.

'It's October. We're about to have our lunch.'

They watch the other passengers being loaded in, until they rise halfway up and can see over the fence and then right above the clock tower, whose bell begins to strike twelve as, with a lurch, they move up to the top.

Angela rattles the carriage. 'This is very dangerous.'

Both girls giggle. Hysterical. It feels suddenly windy, much more exposed than on the ground, even with a tin roof over them. Angela's hair streams, a flame in a hurricane lamp. As the clock's chimes ring out they look down at the fairground and wave, and then down through the bars at the carriage below, and across the town with its Regency and Deco and its wretched tower blocks, and across the Sands. Lisa takes a photo from every direction. Then they drop down and the people who were below them are now above them, at the top, and their view is of girders and spokes.

The wheel revolves smoothly. It clanks and creaks, but the sound is monotonous and restful. Many of the gondolas are unoccupied: they look like empty birdcages. The full ones are like zebra finches on a high-rise balcony, their aviaries suspended from the ceiling, or lashed to the railing with string.

When the ride ends they are at the top, where they remain while the first carriages are unloaded, the cage doors opening and clanging shut before the wheel shifts round, and again and again until they are ushered out.

They go on the dodgems and waltzers and then have lunch in a caff – fried egg sandwiches and chips, with strong tea to follow. Angela wants to find 'Jacques Derrida', so they head into the shopping streets. In the cobbled alleys of the old town they look at the curved-glass shop fronts, the dates in the masonry and the painted brickwork ads, and they browse the displays of junk shops and earmark the good-looking pubs for later. Lisa holds Angela's ice cream as she leafs through the records on a market stall. It has some Scritti Politti but not that song. She gets directions to a second-hand place a few streets away. It's got a wire grille on the windows and black-painted walls. It's shut, but she rings the residential bell and the owner answers.

The stock is piled high and the man is knowledgeable, and soon finds Angela the record. Sipping a coffee and smoking a rollie, he lets her listen to it and she buys it. She leaves the shop triumphantly, brandishing the carrier bag, and he locks up again.

'I've got the words all going round my head now,' she says.

'Cashanova,' says Lisa. 'How you gonna work that in?'

Angela packs 'Jacques Derrida' carefully into her bag.

From the record shop they follow the signs to the Shell Grotto. They pass the Tudor House and take a quick detour into its grounds, making a plan to visit it properly before they leave in the morning.

'Is this where you remember it being?' says Lisa, as they walk up Dane Road.

Angela looks around her at the streets and houses. 'Maybe. Although I think it was less built up, more a quiet country lane.'

'Not much countryside around here though.'

As they approach the grotto, Angela says, 'I don't think this is it.'

'Let's go inside.' Lisa goes in.

'It didn't look like this,' says Angela. 'It had a garden.'

'Could it have been redeveloped?' says Lisa, coming out.

'I remember, very clearly, standing in the lane,' says Angela. 'My brother was leaning on the gatepost. I think we were waiting for my father.'

'Come on in.' Lisa pulls Angela in and pays for their tickets.

'We close at four,' the woman says.

'This isn't it,' says Angela, looking around the walls and shaking her head. 'There are no shells here.'

'The shells are downstairs,' says the ticket attendant, smiling.

'Come on,' says Lisa, taking Angela's hand and pulling her to the stairwell.

Its walls are black and caked with something that looks and smells like slime. A very faint glow of lamps lights the narrow steps. The girls descend the spiral staircase, Lisa leading and Angela following, clutching the back of Lisa's hooded top.

The stuff on the walls is oxidised shells set into blackened mortar. As they climb into the blackness the smell gets stronger — damp and cold dark places and stagnation, with perhaps an undernote of sulphur.

'Phosphorous,' says Lisa.

'This is a cave,' says Angela, as they emerge into the first antechamber.

Low in the wall, recessed shelves sit like catacombs, or votive alcoves. Electric sconces cast a dim light through the passageway. Chambers loom out of the dark, studded with shells from floor to ceiling in patterns of trees and flowers, stars and suns. The sharp edges of mussel shells fan outwards.

Tracing their way around a circular channel, the girls edge past a slightly plump child and his middle-aged parents.

'This definitely isn't it,' says Angela.

'But it's pretty cool, huh?' says Lisa, flicking on her lighter to examine a wall.

They complete the loop and step into a cavern hall, complete with altar.

'The place of sacrifice,' says Lisa, taking a photo.

The boy and his family enter the room.

'Crazy shit,' says Lisa.

The mother looks at them in annoyance.

'D'you think they get bats here, at night?' says Lisa.

Angela shrugs. 'How would they get in? This isn't it. Let's go.'

'Oh come on. It's fun.'

'It isn't fun. I didn't want this. I wanted to see the shell house.'

'You must have misremembered it.'

'I didn't! I didn't misremember it! I didn't imagine it.' Angela is starting to shout. The sound bounces off the walls.

'OK,' says Lisa. 'OK.'

'What are you looking at?' Angela shouts at the boy's parents. And then, at Lisa, 'I remember. I was there.'

'OK.'

'It was a little old lady's cottage. Every surface of the house and garden covered in shells, and garden gnomes made of shells. She'd done it all herself.'

'It sounds lovely.'

Angela starts to sniff. 'I bought a shell ornament there. An owl.'

'Do you still have it?' asks Lisa.

'No,' says Angela, with a sob. 'I don't have it any more.'

Another visitor enters, looks at the tableau, and leaves again quickly.

'We'll find the shell house,' says Lisa, patting Angela's back and trying not to look at the family. 'The woman on the desk will know.'

Upstairs the woman's eyes dart from Lisa to Angela, Angela to Lisa, Lisa to Angela. She doesn't know about a shell house. This is the Shell Grotto, the only one. Lisa thanks her and they go, Lisa pushing Angela out of the door.

Outside, she says, 'Are you sure it was Margate, Angela?'

'Yes it was Margate! I was in secondary school

when I last came, in my first year. A girl from school came with us.'

'Would she remember?'

'We're not in touch.'

They walk back along Dane Road and into King Street.

'What about your family? They'd know.'

Angela looks up. 'My brother. He'd know.'

'Shall we call him?'

In a urine-smelling phone box on the seafront, Lisa holds the door open while Angela dials home, a stack of silver change on the ledge in front of her.

Her brother answers, but he doesn't remember.

'You were nine!' shouts Angela. 'You must remember. A whole house covered in shells, like the gingerbread house. An old lady made it.' And then, after a silence, 'Don't you remember? Michelle came with us in the car. You liked Michelle.'

Angela leans against the phone-box wall, the metal frame digging in.

'Do you remember my owl made of shells? I used to keep it on the windowsill.'

Angela feeds the machine with silver as her brother talks. Through the panes of phone-box glass the sun is beginning to set. Lisa squeezes herself in. The urine smell blooms up as the door springs shut.

'I don't remember anything else,' says Angela to her brother. 'Just the house, and Michelle being there. It's all a blank.'

Angela is pressed into a corner of the booth,

hunched over the receiver away from Lisa, her free hand over her face and in her hair.

Lisa looks outwards at the sunset distorted by glass. She lights a cigarette and, when Angela snaps her fingers, gives one to Angela too. The smell of smoke overtakes the smell of piss.

Over the Harbour Arm, the sky is darkening.

'Nothing,' says Angela. 'Nothing.' And then, 'No. I don't want to talk to her.'

She rings off and swipes at the stack of change, sending it flying, then bursts into tears.

Lisa crouches down and picks up the coins by their edges, holding her breath and trying not to touch the floor. She wraps them in a tissue.

'Let's get out,' she says, and pushes open the door.

Angela stumbles into the fresh air. 'Why doesn't he remember?'

'I suppose nine is quite young.'

'Where could it be?' sobs Angela. 'It must be somewhere.'

'Perhaps the old lady died,' says Lisa.

This just makes Angela cry even harder. She slams her bag against the phone box. It connects with a smash.

The two friends look at each other and Angela stops crying. Her hands shake as she kneels on the pavement and undoes her bag, pulling out the contents, cradling the shattered fragments of 'Jacques Derrida' as she tips them out of their paper sleeve and tries to piece them together on the street.

Lisa watches as Angela fits the pieces over and over again, a jigsaw or a mosaic.

The Tracey Emin show is great, but dense, and needs to be seen in stages. Lisa sits on the shoulder of the Harbour Arm where they ate their chips, where she took the photo. You can walk to the end now (the fingers?), which she doesn't remember being able to do (at least, she doesn't think they did). There's still a fish and chip shop on the front, perhaps the same one, its queue snaking out of the doorway. Though tempted, Lisa has opted this time for an overpriced panino from the Turner café, and a decaf latte.

In the new tourist information office situated in the Droit House on the Arm (now adorned with an Emin neon), Lisa scours the brochures. At the counter she asks casually about the shell cottage. 'You mean the Shell Grotto,' says the woman, handing her a leaflet.

'I'm not sure,' says Lisa. 'I'm looking for something from the 1980s. A house covered in shells? A kind of folly — outsider art.'

'This is the one,' says the woman, pointing at the Shell Grotto picture. Lisa smiles and thanks her.

Wandering out of the Droit House, she happens upon Mark Wallinger's shed: the *Sinema Amnesia*. Unsure whether it's open, she crosses over, finds the doorway, and peers in. The elderly usherette beckons her and gestures the seat. Lisa sits down in the black box. In front of her, the fourth wall appears to be a fine metal scrim, through which the sea is visible. She looks out at the view for a while, and then around the black walls of the cinema booth: there is nothing else.

'I don't get it,' she says.

'It's yesterday's view.' The usherette hands her a flyer. 'You're watching what happened twenty-four hours ago.'

Lisa gets up and peers at the wall in front of her. It's not a scrim: it's a projection. She laughs. 'It looks exactly the same as today.'

The woman shrugs and smiles. 'Doesn't always,' she says.

Lisa gazes out at yesterday's sea and sky. They're blue, and calm, and full of sunshine.

The Man in the Pool

Shaun Levin

I don't like the way the man looks at my son, the way he stares, no matter where we are or what Julian's wearing, but particularly here where it's warm and in the evenings we swim in the hotel's indoor pool. The man has no idea how young Julian is; if he knew, he'd be ashamed to be ogling a fifteen-year-old boy. My son is oblivious, doing his laps, drying himself, texting his friends, mildly embarrassed to be here with his father and me, on holiday in Spain. We're here for a week, six nights, to get away from the fire that burnt down our business. When we get back, we'll start over. Julian knows nothing about the fire; we agreed to tell him when we get back to London. He's been doing well at school, top marks in Spanish, so this trip to Almería is his treat.

The pool's big enough for ten strokes per length and both the man and my son cover the pool from one end to the other in just a couple of breaths; it's as if they've silently agreed to race each other. The man must be my age, maybe a bit older, his back broad, his hair dark and straight, shining when wet. My son could be his son, but the man does not look at him the way a father looks at a son. The sound of their hands and feet against the water echoes in the enclosure. My husband's upstairs in the room reading before dinner, detective novels and crime thrillers, books that are easy on the mind.

'I want to forget,' he says.

The fire came out of nowhere. It could have been a fuse or the toaster-oven left on overnight. The reason isn't important; there'd been a fire and the place had burnt down. The fire engines had arrived after we did – too late to save anything. The whole thing is a blessing in disguise, although I do not say this to my husband. This is our first holiday in ten years, and when we get home we can make big changes, use the insurance money to do what we really want to do, leave the city, move somewhere quiet.

I can tell by the way the man moves his head, as if to breathe, that he is staring at Julian's body, angling his head to the side, keeping it underwater when he passes my son.

Julian stops at the shallow end and stands up.

'Claudette,' he says.

'Yes, son,' I say, the word sweet in my mouth.

'Is it time to eat yet?' he says.

The man keeps swimming, somersaulting with

each turn, pushing himself off the side with such force I'm afraid he'll collide with Julian's legs as he stands there in the pool calling out to me.

After dinner, my husband and I make love. His body is firm and strong and solid and he smells of salt and coconut oil. When we kiss I taste the evening's salmon on his breath; his mouth is big and his tongue is heavy and everything about him is warm and determined. I wonder if this is the kind of body Julian will have when he grows up; for now he is slim and agile, taller than boys his age, taller than my husband. His height makes people think he's older than he is. In pubs they serve him without questions.

We lie here and the smell of the sea is comforting, the sound of the waves, white strips of them flopping onto the shore. Julian is asleep at the far end of the corridor and for the moments that this worries me, he might as well be on the other side of the world, teaching English in the Andes, backpacking through Tanzania, wrenched from me. The man in the pool moves back and forth across my field of vision, like a shark, like something circling its prey.

'You're restless,' my husband says.

'It's too humid to sleep,' I say.

'Turn on the air conditioning,' he says.

'I'll be fine,' I say.

He kisses my cheek and turns onto his side, this man who will sleep through anything. It is November and the nights are cool, though the days are still warm and good for the beach, the sun bright and hot so that by the end of the day we are tired and the cool breeze is pleasant on the skin. As my husband's breathing slows, I listen to the quiet intake and exhalation of air, feel myself drifting off, soothed by the rise and fall next to me and the sound of waves, and I wish for my son this kind of companionship and the calming sea and I imagine stroking his head and whispering, sleep, my baby boy, like I've whispered to him many times before.

In the morning we eat alone, my husband and I, a breakfast of pineapple cubes, toast with jam and cheese, fresh coffee, and I don't mention anything about the man who looks at our son in that way, even though he's sitting opposite us, close to the big windows, the sun shining in over the sea and onto his table. I like the ease of this place, as if we're in North Africa, the sun so bright that even in autumn it bleaches the buildings, parches everything, peeling plaster, dust from the desert. The bougainvillea grows wild.

In today's paper there is an article about a girl who jumped from the window of her hotel in Prague. The article says her father raped her several times a year from when she was five until she turned thirteen. Two days ago was her nineteenth birthday; three days ago she was about to win a chess tournament. People blamed the stress of the impending finals, then they found a recording she'd made one night with friends, all of them drunk, and her voice recounting what her father had done to her.

How does a father not kill himself after that, follow in his daughter's footsteps and leap from a window to the pavement? The girl died in a foreign city where she wouldn't be recognised by passers-by, like she could walk off the face of the earth, like she'd never been born.

I will do everything to make sure my son knows he is adored.

'You know we love you,' I'd said to him.

'Yes, Claudette,' he said. 'I know that.'

We were sitting in the lobby last night after he'd come out of the so-called Business Centre where he'd been checking emails. The guests were playing bingo, a mixed crowd in their sixties and seventies on a package holiday, Spanish tourists from somewhere else in Spain. They made me happy, this band of pensioners, cocooning me in a language I don't understand, lulled by the clean smell of chlorine from the decorative pools in the reception area, lively Spanish music and the sound of birds in the aviaries by the entrance. The young bingo caller with her straight black hair and tight orange top shifting her gaze when Julian came towards me, smiling at him.

We ordered *dos cervezas* and a *jamón* and cheese sandwich from the waiter.

'The bus leaves at ten tomorrow,' I said. 'It'll be a fun trip.'

'I'm fine just staying here.'

'Are you happy, Julian?' I said.

'What do you mean?'

'Here,' I said. 'In general.'

'Oh, definitely,' he said. 'Ecstatic.'

We both laughed, an hysterical kind of laughter, for the absurdity of the question, here, so far from home. The laughing melted something, softened us, and I felt the warmth that comes with having known each other for so long. I have known this boy all his life. Which is when I told him about the fire.

'We'll be making changes.'

'What kind of changes?' he said.

'We'll talk about it, the three of us,' I said. 'Nothing is final.'

The waiter approached and we ordered two more bottles of beer, and when they came they were cold and sweet and we drank in silence. I said something about the young woman in charge of the bingo and Julian shrugged me off, told me to stop. When the game was over the barman turned the music down and the old people went back to their rooms, the stage stood empty like something abandoned; the young woman had disappeared, smuggled out unnoticed by her audience.

'Call the boy,' my husband says. 'He'll miss breakfast.'

'Have you seen this story?'

'You know I haven't,' he says.

'Here.' And I hand him the paper.

I open a serviette and wrap up two croissants and little tubs of jam and butter.

'The bus leaves in an hour,' I say.

The waiters smile and say *buenos días* when I leave the dining room and take the lift up to the third floor where my son is just waking up.

The bus from Almería to the old town of Mojácar crosses through the desert, past roundabouts similar to the ones in Baghdad we saw on the news when soldiers entered the city. In the middle of the roundabouts are white arches and statues, large stick men, bright white against the pale blue sky, like a child's drawing of a man, a long line for the body, two shorter ones for the arms and legs, a circle for the head, and above the head, a semi-circle like an umbrella or an archer's bow. The desert is vast and open, and the dry air through the window is warm on my face.

I was fourteen when it happened. He was older, from another school. I'd crossed a line, had started smoking and when we did it I asked for a cigarette. It felt like the right thing to do. An actress on a bed in a movie. We smoked without saying anything and he didn't ask if I was okay or how it was. He was slight, not much bigger than me and I vowed I'd always be with men into whom I could disappear, who would shield me, and with David, my husband, I have found that.

In the paper they said it was always just after her birthday, unlucky to be born when the nights are too long, when darkness keeps people at home and allows things like this to happen. How does anyone write the story of a child entered by her father? Are men allowed to write these stories after the things they do?

She was not a virgin on the first day of school.

How does one continue after a sentence like that?

And if the father is to blame, then others are to blame. Let them all queue up on the window ledge of the hotel in Prague and get ready, like divers, to hit the ground. Take them with you, precious girl. Take them all. Your father who did it while your mother slept – or in the mornings when she was at work, always in your bed, his hand over your mouth, his breath sweet from cinnamon biscuits.

The cinnamon stink of Christmas.

Death was the girl's only escape. She jumped to save herself.

Before the bus turns left towards the beach, we get off and head into Mojácar la Vieja, to the public fountain at the foot of the hill. Water spouts jut out from the wall, and the locals come to fill their bottles and plastic containers from the mountain spring. The water pours out in thick cold streams and it's when I bend down to drink that my back clenches, a sharp pain from my tailbone and down my leg.

'Claudette,' my husband says. 'Sit for a bit.'

'It's better to move,' I say. 'Let's keep walking.'

So we climb towards the top of the old town, the steep and winding streets, and stop for a while at the observation point to look out over the desert, the dusty shrubs, construction work everywhere, and in the distance rows of white houses close to the shore, and beyond that – the sea. Julian walks ahead of us, like it's a race to the top. There's a film of sweat on his arms and the back of his neck. His steps are buoyant, light, and suddenly I want to collapse onto a bench and weep, wail to have brought something into the world that is so pure and destined to leave. I have given life to this boy just so he can teach me lessons in grief and loss.

'I told him about the fire,' I say to David.

'How did he take it?' he says.

'I said there'll be changes.'

'What kind of changes?'

'I don't know,' I say. 'I honestly don't know.'

'Are you okay, Claude?' he says.

'It's good we've come away for a bit,' I say.

In one of the gift shops at the top of the village, we buy fridge magnets with little versions of the stick man, the same shape as the statues on the traffic roundabouts. *For good luck*, the woman in the shop tells us, and we notice on the way down that the houses have similar tiles on their walls to ward off evil spirits. David and I hold hands, and I want to give my other hand to Julian, to be flanked by my two men, but I know it is too late for that.

'Somewhere like this place,' I say to my husband. 'It's nice here.'

'It is,' he says. 'And far and foreign, and miles away from anything.'

'That's a good thing.'

'It's good if that's what a person wants,' he says.

'I think I just want to go home now,' I say.

The bus drops us back at the hotel with an hour to spare before dinner. Julian wants his evening swim but there isn't time and the pain in my back has worn me out.

'Just a quick one,' he says.

'And then straight to dinner,' I say.

'Yes, Mother,' he says.

'I'm warning you,' I say, wagging my finger at him.

'Come rest your back,' David says.

The room is like a homecoming. We have emerged from the desert into an oasis, the bed made, the room warm from the day and with the glass doors closed the quiet is soothing. My husband says that if there's one good thing about this place it's the abundance of fish; he's never eaten so much fish in his life. I say I'd be happy never to leave this room, just to lie here, the sea and traffic humming beyond the glass, and the rustling of the pages as he reads his book.

'I want them to move Julian to a closer room,' I say.

'We can ask,' David says.

'Or we could move to that end of the passage,' I say.

'What are you worried about?'

'About Julian,' I say. 'I'm worried.'

'He can look after himself,' he says.

'No, he can't,' I say. 'He's fifteen.'

'Jesus, Claude,' he says. 'I was having sex at his age.'

'And?' I say. 'So was I.'

'No, you weren't,' he says, and laughs.

'Can you just call them and ask?' I say.

'At fifteen?' he says. 'Really?'

'Do you notice how some men look at him?' I say.

'What are you talking about?'

'This guy in the pool in the evenings. He stares at Julian.'

'He's a good-looking boy.'

'He's fifteen,' I say.

It happened just that once with the older boy and for a long time after that never again with anyone.

'What do you think of that guy who eats alone?' I say.

'Which one?' he says.

My husband is not the most perceptive. When it's dinner time he's focused on his dinner. I know he's trying not to make a big fuss of things, as if he can't see what has actually happened, this burning down of the business two years after we set it up, the shop, the machines, computers, desks, new chairs that we'd bought just a couple of weeks ago.

'He's got a smarmy dirty-old-man look,' I say.

'If *he's* old,' he says. 'What would you call me?'

'What's he doing here? What's a man doing alone in a place like this?'

'Let's ask him,' he says.

'Don't,' I say.

'He doesn't look like a paedophile,' David says.

'What does that mean?'

'He doesn't look like he'd make a pass at Julian,' he says. 'Like he'd touch him or something.'

'I can't listen to this,' I say. 'This is obscene.'

The next morning at breakfast, walking with our plates from the buffet, my husband stops at the man's table.

'Can we join you?' he says.

'Of course,' the man says.

He's French. His dark hair brushes against his shoulders when he glances around the room, mildly surprised; there are empty tables. Still, he moves his plate of toast and a small jug of milk to make room for us.

'Only the two of you?' he says.

'What do you mean?' I say.

'Your son?'

'The lazy teenager,' my husband says.

'Growing pains,' the man says. 'They need to sleep.'

'He's grown enough,' I say.

'Have you hurt your back?' the man says.

'It comes and goes,' I say, my gaze fixed on my plate, the scrambled eggs, the rinds of bacon.

Jean-Luc is an acupuncturist and a massage therapist; he comes to Spain once a year to see clients at a local clinic. He tells us his son will be arriving from Lyon later in the morning; he's collecting him from the airport. This is their holiday time together.

'We'll be home the day after tomorrow,' I say. 'I've already booked a session.'

'It's no problem,' he says. 'I am happy to see you.'

'Go,' my husband says. 'We've got a cramped flight ahead of us.'

'Fine,' I say. 'But no needles.'

He stands at our table smiling down at us, and the man smiles up at him.

'The lazy son,' my husband says.

Julian holds out his hand to the man and says, 'Hey, Jean-Luc.'

'You ready for a rematch, young man?' he says.

Later that afternoon, when my husband and I meet

Jean-Luc in the indoor pool area, there is a boy strapped to a high-backed wheelchair facing the pool. His eyes shift when we come into his field of vision. The place is hot and humid from the heated pool and the sun shining in through the glass walls.

'Would you mind keeping an eye on Serge?' Jean-Luc says to my husband.

'Sure,' David says. 'Gladly.'

'He likes being read to,' Jean-Luc says.

'Does he speak English?' I say.

'No,' Jean-Luc smiles. 'But he likes it anyway.'

'Detective novels?' David says to the boy. '*Romans policiers*?'

The boy smiles at him, his mouth full of teeth.

Jean-Luc and I go up in the lift together, not completely like strangers, as if there is a bond between us, a shared experience, even though this is the first time we're alone together. He makes light conversation, asks how long I've been seeing my massage therapist, if I've ever had my back X-rayed. My answers are short and cautious, they feel like accusations. I don't ask about his son, about the boy's mother. A handsome boy with a healthy head of hair, blue eyes, a version of his father, misaligned.

When we enter the room Jean-Luc's voice becomes soft. The lights have been dimmed and the curtains are closed despite us being too high up for anyone to see in. The massage table is set up between his bed and the desk. Jean-Luc turns to light a candle and switches on some music, a sitar, the soft drumming of a tabla.

'Whatever is comfortable for you,' he says.

So I remove my clothes, my underwear, and climb up onto the table while his gaze is still averted. The towel he uses is warm against my back, my buttocks, and Jean-Luc presses his palms into my shoulder blades, and down, peels the towel to one side and moves to my legs, my shins and calves and with warmed oil kneads my flesh upwards, pushing everything back into my body. His touch is firm and confident, and all the while I can feel his eyes on me, my legs, my back, his hands in constant motion, the soft strings of the sitar, the drumming of fingertips, and because I cannot move and I have chosen to be here, the only option I have is to surrender to his touch.

ABOUT THE AUTHORS

RUBY COWLING was born in West Yorkshire and now lives in London. In 2014 she was awarded both *The White Review* Short Story Prize and the London Short Story Prize. Her work has appeared in various anthologies and magazines including: *The View From Here, Punchnel's, The Letters Page, Unthology 4* and (in audio format) *4'33"* and *Bound Off*.

USCHI GATWARD was born in East London and lives there now. Her stories have appeared or are forthcoming in *Best British Short Stories 2015* (Salt), the *Bristol Short Story Prize Anthology Volume 6, Brittle Star, Southword* and *Structo*. She once went to Margate with a girl called Angela, but the rest is fiction.

SHAUN LEVIN is the author of *Seven Sweet Things, A Year of Two Summers* and *Snapshots of the Boy*. His short stories appear in the anthologies *The Slow Mirror and Other Stories: New Fiction by Jewish Writers, Modern South African Stories,* and *Boyfriends from Hell,* amongst others. He teaches creative writing and is the deviser of Writing Maps. See more at shaunlevin.com and writingmaps.com.

JENNIFER OBIDIKE is an American writer living and working in London. She is currently a Flight 1000 Associate for Spread the Word. She has volunteered for numerous writing organisations across London including Spread the Word, the Royal Society of Literature and the Ministry of Stories. In 2012, she founded and facilitated Wine Women Words, London, a writing workshop for women to share and feedback on fiction. She has an MFA in Creative Writing from the New School, a university in New York City.

SANYA SEMAKULA was born in Uganda but grew up in England. She is now a London-based short story writer and poet. In 2015 she was awarded the gold award for short fiction from Creative Futures. Her work can also be found online at the quarterly magazine *LossLit*. As well as being a Flight 1000 Associate at Spread the Word, she is also working on a collection of short stories.

COLETTE SENSIER was born in Brighton and lives in London. Her poetry has been widely anthologised, with *Skinless*, her debut collection, published in 2014. She completed a novel, *The Inhabitants*, during a Spread the Word mentoring scheme and a Creative Writing MA at the University of East Anglia. She works in marketing and communications for a small charity.

JANET H SWINNEY was born and grew up in the North East of England and now lives in London. She worked for many years in post-16 education in roles that ranged from practitioner to inspector. She has had stories shortlisted in the Fish International Short Story Contest and highly commended in the Bristol Short Story Prize. Her story 'The Map of Bihar' was the editor's choice in the Eric Hoffer Prose Award 2013 and appeared in *Best New Writing 2013* (Hopewell Publications). She has recently completed her first collection of short fiction. She has travelled widely in India, and supports the development organisations 'Womankind Worldwide' and 'Impact India'.

STEPHANIE VICTOIRE was born in London to a Mauritian family. In 2010 she graduated from London Metropolitan University with a BA in Creative Writing. In March 2013, she was accepted onto the Almasi League Writers Programme, run by author Courttia Newland. In October 2014, she was mentored by author Kerry Hudson, for the *WoMentoring Project* and in January 2015, her short story, 'Animal Ball', was published in the American literary magazine, *¶ilcrow & Dagger.* In February 2015, she performed a reading of her folk tale, '*Shanty* ', at Almasi League's showcase event, UNCOVERED. She has recently finished writing her collection of fairy and folk tales, *The Other World, It Whispers,* and is now working on a novel.

KATIE WILLIS was a ballet dancer until illness came along and forced a change of direction. As her world shrank to an inside dark space, she wrote grown-up fairy tales in order to find a way out. Her characters reside on the margins of society, and that is where her illness continues to take her, into uncharted borderlands. She now lives happily in west London and has been longlisted for the Bristol Short Story Prize. She came second in the 2014 Puffin Review fairy tale contest with her story, 'Mr Forrester Has Wings'. She is currently completing a novel (shortlisted in the Brit Writers Awards) and working on producing a body of short stories. 'The Passenger' is her first short story to be published in an anthology.

ABOUT SPREAD THE WORD

Spread the Word is London's writer development agency, a National Portfolio Organisation of Arts Council England. It is based in the vibrant theatre and community arts centre The Albany in Deptford. We are interested in the artistic and social impact of creative writing, and work with writers and diverse communities on a wide range of long-term and one-off projects and events. We provide high quality, low cost opportunities for writers to improve their craft and develop their careers.

We identify and support talented writers from a diversity of backgrounds and encourage as many people as possible to try creative writing as a means of self-expression. Some of the projects we run include the Young Poet Laureate for London project, Flight 1000, Writing the Future, London Short Story Prize and the London Short Story Festival.

web: spreadtheword.org.uk
twitter: @stwevents
facebook: facebook.com/spreadthewordwriters

CPSIA information can be obtained
at www.ICGtesting.com
Printed in the USA
LVOW11s1435030417
529436LV00001B/370/P